ALSO BY LISA YEE

Millicent Min, Girl Genius
Stanford Wong Flunks Big-Time
So Totally Emily Ebers

Bobby vs. Girls (Accidentally)
Bobby the Brave (Sometimes)

Absolutely Maybe

WARP SPEED

LISA YEE

SCHOLASTIC INC.

NEW YORK TORONTO LONDON AUCKLAND
SYDNEY MEXICO CITY NEW DELHI HONG KONG

Special thanks to Matt Cunningham for sharing his infinite knowledge of *Star Wars* and Batman; Ed Masessa, who explained why wearing a red shirt is not recommended when appearing on *Star Trek*; and Curtis Sponsler, my projection-booth expert extraordinaire. Also, a shout-out to Benny for going over this book with me when he could have been skateboarding.

ISBN 978-0-545-39119-1

Arthur A. Levine Books hardcover edition published by Arthur A. Levine Books, an imprint of Scholastic Inc., March 2011

12 11 10 9 8 7 6 5 4 3 2 1   11 12 13 14 15 16/0

Printed in the U.S.A.   40

First Scholastic paperback printing, September 2011

This book is dedicated
to Arthur Levine.

"Marley was dead, to begin with."

Marley was dead, to begin with? What kind of stupid opening line is that? *A Christmas Carol* is supposed to be some sort of classic novel about a ghost, but I didn't have to read another word to know that it was a classic waste of my time.

My name is Marley. You know, like that famous dog. However, my mother claims I was named after Crandall Marley, the writer whose book swept the literary world . . . after he committed suicide. So there you have it. I share my name with a dog, a dead guy, and a ghost. Is it any wonder my life sucks?

The sun is starting to set as I approach the school parking lot and spot a bunch of donkeys. They don't look very happy. I'm sure they'd rather be out in the woods, or on a farm, or wherever donkeys hang out — but instead they're going to be forced to play basketball.

I'm not a basketball fan. I don't even know why I'm here. I hate basketball. There's still fifteen minutes before the Hee-Haw Game begins, but as I make my way into the gym I can see that it's already packed. I spot Ramen off in the corner by himself. He's my best friend by default, since neither of us really has any other friends. It looks like he finally got a new *Star Wars* T-shirt. I duck behind some kids before he sees me. I don't feel like listening to him talk about *Star Wars* all night. A guy has his limits.

As I push my way up the bleachers, I get punched in the arm three times. This started last year. Some guy hit me for no reason, and now he and his two idiot sidekicks do it all the time. I call them the Gorn, after the evil slow-moving beasts who first appeared in "Arena," *Star Trek*: *The Original Series* (a.k.a. *TOS*), Season One, Episode 18. The biggest Gorn is the leader. His head looks like a giant pink grapefruit, he's got a beak nose, and he's missing a front tooth. The middle Gorn is missing part of his left eyebrow. He hits the hardest. The smallest Gorn is crazy scary, laughs like a little girl, and appears to be missing a brain. All of them have shaved heads and wear letterman jackets with no letters on them. They used to play football, but got kicked off the team for not playing by the rules. Each time any of them lands a punch, they high-five. Forget touchdowns — just hit Marley instead.

From up here I can see swarms of kids buzzing around, checking each other out. The eighth graders control the left side of the gym. Some of them are bigger than the teachers. The football players are huddled together near the front door. (At our school, the only thing bigger than football is basketball. Basketball is huge.) The kids who look like preschoolers are the incoming sixth graders. They're really short and don't even try to disguise that they're thrilled out of their minds to have finally made it to middle school. Everything is exciting to them. The lockers! The cafeteria! Tiggy the Tiger, our school mascot!

The row I'm sitting in is full of popular kids. No one seems to mind that I'm here. For once I feel sort of cool. Coach Martin stands in the middle of the gym. Why are all the P.E. teachers out of shape? He adjusts his Dodgers cap, then blows his whistle until everyone quiets down. Coach Martin loves that whistle. I'll bet he sleeps with it. I'll bet he blows his whistle when he takes a dump.

"Tonight's the big Hee-Haw Game," he shouts into the microphone. There's a high-pitched squeal. Everyone covers their ears. Coach Martin is standing too close to the loudspeakers, causing them to re-amp and give off feedback. He takes a few steps back. "It's the A-Team against the faculty, and as you know, everyone rides donkeys. Hey, guys," he says, motioning to the basketball players, "if you give us teachers a break we'll go easy on you when school starts tomorrow."

The crowd laughs like he's said something funny. I try laughing too, and turn to Dean Hoddin, who's on my left. We sat next to each other in science last year and were partners on the earthquake project. I did most of the work. Dean's popular, meaning he can't walk down the hallway without a dozen kids saying hi to him.

"Coach Martin's pretty funny, don't you think?" I say to Dean. Maybe we'll be partners again this year in some class. It went pretty well last year and he was thrilled when we got an A. He even said to me, "You're okay."

Dean stares at me blankly. Maybe he didn't hear me. The acoustics in this gym are awful. Everyone's talking and Coach is tapping on the microphone. I repeat louder, "Coach Martin's pretty funny, don't you think so, Dean?"

"Do we know each other?" he asks, loud enough for everyone around us to hear.

I feel my face heat up. "Sorry, I thought you were someone else," I mumble.

As Coach Martin babbles on, the girl on my right taps me on the shoulder. Everyone thinks Julie is the most beautiful girl at school. From the way she acts, it's clear she agrees with them.

"Do you mind if we change seats so I can sit next to Dean?" Julie asks as she flings her blonde hair over her shoulder. She used to do this all the time in math. It's her signature move.

"Oh. Oh, yeah, sure," I tell her. I have to admit she *is* beautiful. My heart is racing, and I hate myself for that. "We had math together last year."

"Whatever," she says as she scoots next to Dean. I sit down on her other side.

Someone else taps me on the shoulder. "Do you mind changing seats so I can sit next to Julie?" one of her followers asks. She smiles at me and bats her eyelashes, then blows a bubble-gum bubble almost as big as her head.

"Sure," I say as the bubble pops. She gives me another smiles as she stuffs the gum back into her mouth and changes seats with me.

This happens four more times, until I'm sitting at the end of the bleacher. It's so crowded that I'm almost falling off. I hear laughter and look around to see what's so funny. Then it hits me.

Everyone is laughing at me. I'm the joke.

I laugh too, like I'm in on it instead of being made fun of again. Besides, what are my choices? If I didn't do anything, they'd keep laughing, and if I cried, well . . . that's not an option.

I climb to the top row of the bleachers. I can see better from up here anyway. I reach into my pocket. Yep, I've still got my Captain Kirk action figure. Kirk's so cool. He's courageous and confident, and he commands total respect from his crew on the USS *Enterprise*.

Coach Martin introduces the basketball A-Team members. Stanford Wong is last. He gets the biggest roar from the crowd, even though he's the only seventh grader on a team full of eighth graders. Stanford's some sort of hero just because he can throw a ball through a hoop. Big deal. Those donkeys play basketball too and nobody treats them like royalty.

I remember when Stanford was a nobody. We used to be best friends, if you can believe that. It was long before he ever picked up a basketball. We could talk *Star Trek* for hours. I've even been to Stanford's house. He has one of those refrigerators that make ice, plus there's a two-car garage. We don't even own a car. A lot of years have passed since Stanford Wong has invited me to his house. Now he pretends he doesn't even know me — not that I care.

I retrieve a small red leather-bound notebook from my pocket. On *Star Trek*, Captain Kirk records his voice onto his Captain's Log to keep track of what's happening on his missions. I sort of do the same thing, only instead of recording my voice, I write and sometimes doodle. My Captain's Log is all worn out. At the start of every new year, I write a word that describes me. In the past I've written "hopeful" and "adequate."

invisible

The basketball game is actually pretty entertaining. Stanford is the best player. He scores a last-minute shot that's unbelievable. Even I'm cheering, until I realize it's not like he cured cancer or anything.

Afterward Stanford waves to the crowd. Just who does he think he is? When he scans the bleachers, our eyes lock. Then he does something I can't believe. Stanford Wong gives me the Vulcan salute. It was our signal when we were little kids. When we were friends.

Slowly, I raise my hand to return the salute. Stanford starts toward me, but is mobbed by fans. Then he's gone.

I probably just imagined the Vulcan salute. Or that we were ever friends.

I'm almost home. We live in the upstairs apartment of the Rialto Theater. I reach for my Captain's Log to record an entry . . . but wait . . . my Captain's Log is missing!

Quickly, I retrace my steps. By the time I get back to the gym, it's empty. I race up the bleachers to where I was sitting. I look everywhere but can't find it. It's nowhere, like it vaporized.

"How was the basketball game?" my mother asks. She's stirring the vegetable soup on the stove and I can smell the onions. It's pitch-black in the kitchen, so I turn on the light.

"It was okay." I pour myself some lemonade and drain the glass.

Mom brushes the hair off my face. "Almost time for a haircut," she notes. Her fingers flitter across my brow. "You seem worried."

"I'm not," I tell her as I pull away. Even though she's blind, it's impossible to hide anything from her.

"Did Stanford Wong play?" Mom asks. She's wearing a blue shirt and a denim skirt. All her clothes are blue or white, so she can mix and match. With her shoulder-length black hair and no-nonsense style, my mother looks like Bonnie Bedelia in *Heart Like a Wheel*. Dad showed the movie in the Rialto last year during his Speed Week Marathon.

"Yeah, Stanford played," I tell her.

"How did he do?"

"Great, like always."

"You should invite Stanford to dinner sometime," my

mother says as she slices a thick wedge of her homemade bread. "He used to love my cooking." She ladles the soup into a big bowl and I watch the steam rise, then disappear. "It seems like forever since he's been here."

That's because it *has* been forever, I start to tell her, but then stop myself. Why waste the energy? Stanford Wong is never coming back. Besides, I don't have time to think about him. I'll bet someone stole my Captain's Log and is reading it right now. "Loser," they're probably saying. "Marley Sandelski is a loser."

"Take this to your dad for me," Mom says, handing me a tray. "Be careful not to spill."

My father is in the projection booth of the Rialto. It's cramped and loud, but I love it. When I was a baby and had trouble sleeping, my mother would bring me here, knowing that the steady purr of the projector would lull me to sleep.

The previews are just ending. My father cues the theater music, then closes the heavy red velvet curtains that flank the screen down below. There are only a handful of people in the Rialto tonight. Still, he makes sure they get a good show. Dad fades the lights, then, three . . . two . . . one . . . the curtains reopen and the feature film begins. I hand him the soup. He eases down into his swivel chair and cups the bowl in his hands. "Tell your mother thank you," he says as he dips a piece of the bread into it. "Want to stay? It's *Casablanca*."

"I'll stay until Victor Lazlo shows up," I tell him. I like Victor Lazlo. He's a man of mystery. "Then I have to get ready for school."

"I almost forgot," Dad says. "You start seventh grade tomorrow. Are you looking forward to it?"

"No."

"Marley," he says, "it'll be fine. You'll see. Just be yourself."

Excuse me? Being myself all these years is the reason I'm a nobody.

I go to my room and reach for the Captain Kirk cookie jar on the top shelf. Twenty, forty, sixty . . . I have over $130. This year the Super *Star Trek* Convention is in Los Angeles and only a twenty-minute bus ride away. Can you guess who's going? That's right. Me. $130 is enough for a ticket, and food, and even a signed poster or two. It's the one thing I've been looking forward to.

I put the money back and get ready for seventh grade, which basically means I sit on my bed and dread tomorrow. Will I get shoved into the lockers? Will I get punched between classes? Will I get spit on? Oh, wait. The real questions are: How often will I get shoved into the lockers? How many times will I get punched between classes? How much spit will land on me?

I close my eyes and try to imagine what tomorrow would be like if I lived in an alternate universe. As I drift off to sleep, I can see myself walking down the hall-way. Everyone knows who I am. I'm no longer invisible. Instead, I am a somebody.

3.

All around me, kids are greeting each other like they're long-lost relatives — smiling, laughing, slapping each other on the back. When Dean Hoddin and Stanford Wong stroll to their lockers, everyone says hi to them. Stanford gets the most hellos. I count seventeen before I stop. He says hi back like it's no big deal. But it is a big deal. When someone says hi to you, it means that they see you and that you exist. In *Star Trek: Enterprise*, the "Vanishing Point" episode, Hoshi starts becoming invisible. Before long, when no one can see her even though she can see them, they just assume she's dead.

"Hi, Marley!"

I whip around, then the smile slides off my face. "Oh, it's you," I say to Ramen.

"Nice to see you too," he answers. It looks like Ramen's wearing his new *Star Wars* shirt again. His old one had holes in it, making it look like R2-D2 had been shot. I'm wearing my second-best Mr. Spock T-shirt, the one with the spaghetti stain on it that looks like blood, but obviously not Vulcan blood, since everyone knows that's green.

Spock's my favorite. He doesn't get all emotional like some of the others on the USS *Enterprise*. Don't get me wrong, I like Scotty and the rest of the gang, and Captain Kirk is the best. But Spock, well, he's so logical and always in control of his emotions. I'm always trying to channel my inner Spock, and whenever I'm stuck I always ask myself WWSD — *What would Spock do?* Today I have a Spock action figure in my pocket for good luck. I usually have one of the *Star Trek* crew with me, in case I need backup.

"Who do you have for homeroom?" Ramen asks. He stares at a crumpled piece of paper. "I have McKenna."

"Yeah, me too," I tell him.

We head to class together. People assume we're best friends because he's into *Star Wars* and I'm into *Star Trek*. How bogus is that? I could never truly respect someone who's delusional enough to think *Star Wars* is the greatest. Everyone knows that without *Star Trek* there'd be no *Star Wars*.

I'm really into the original *Trek* series. Not to be a snob, but the later shows and the movies just don't cut it. I mean, they're still great and I've seen them all. But the original series, well, it doesn't get any better than that.

"Good morning, class!" It's our teacher. She's way too peppy to be taken seriously. Even her hair bounces when she walks. Still, everyone sits up and quiets down. This won't last. I can already tell that she's one of those teachers who wants to be "friends" with their students. My theory is validated when I notice she's wearing red Converse high-tops as if to say, "I may be your teacher, but really I'm cool like you."

"Hello, I'm Ms. McKenna. This should be an exciting year for all of us. I'm going to be your homeroom teacher and, for many of you, your history teacher too."

I check my class schedule. Yep, I have McKenna for history. Great.

As she blabbers on about the school rules, I zone out. I wish I had my Captain's Log. I wonder where it went. Does someone have it? ". . . and so," Ms. McKenna is still rambling, "if you need to talk to me for any reason, you can. I'm here for you —"

Oh please. I give her two weeks before she stops being all bubbly and starts to pop. I check out the other kids in the room. Most of them I recognize, even though I don't know them personally. Digger Ronster glares at me when he catches me staring at him. He has icy blue eyes and flaming red hair. The corners of his lips curl into the kind of smile I associate with mass murderers.

Julie sits near me. I watch as she flips her hair over her shoulder. "Stop staring at me. It's creepy," she says to me loudly. Everyone around us laughs. I wonder if Ms. McKenna would mark me down if I ran out of the class right now.

I somehow get through P.E., math, and English when at last the noon bell rings. Julie and Dean Hoddin greet their admirers in the hallway. James Ichida, a kid from the track team, seems to have a lot of friends too. When I retrieve my lunch from my locker, something wet slides down my arm. I turn around as a couple of boys laugh and run away.

Okay . . . the first spit — I guess that means that the school year has officially started. I wipe it off and head to the broken bench near the parking lot. It's just far enough from the tree so that you can either be in the shade or sit on the bench, but not both. The tree looks like one side got lopped off, and it leans to the left as if it were surrendering. Over the years, kids have carved things into the trunk. Names, swear words, a happy face. Ramen and I call it the "Tragic Tree." The busted sprinkler under it has created a permanent mud pit.

Ramen's standing in the mud, chowing down on his beloved noodles. His real name is Luke Serrano, but his nickname is Ramen because he eats Top Ramen noodles every day. "Why not?" he says. "They have lots of different flavors — shrimp, beef, chicken . . ." He's like a walking commercial. At the beginning of fifth grade, we were the same size. Now here we are, two years later, and I'm almost a foot taller than him.

It feels like it's 100 degrees. I'm sweating and my arm hurts. So far today I was slugged twice in the morning, once by the Gorn leader and once by the middle Gorn. Then, right before lunch, I got slugged again, this time by the small Gorn. They are three for three. Woo hoo.

During class I watched my bruises form. They're still in the early stages, but eventually they will go from red to purplish blue to green and then yellow. If they weren't so painful, they would be pretty.

I hate the Gorn.

The rest of the day drags, but I get through it thinking about the *Star Trek* Convention. Over 10,000 Trekkers attend, and it's packed with *Star Trek* celebrities, *Star Trek* seminars, *Star Trek* memorabilia, *Star Trek* costume contests, *Star Trek* screenings, *Star Trek* everything. Just thinking about it makes me happy. Why can't I attend Starfleet Academy like Kirk and Spock did instead of Rancho Rosetta Middle School?

Sixth period finally rolls around. Sixth period's okay. In fact, sixth period is the only good thing about school.

Before we even sit down, Mr. Jiang scowls and says, "I hope you geekazoids are ready to work this year." He peers over the top of his glasses and looks me up and down. "Marley Sandelski, how is it possible that you're even skinnier than last year? You've grown again, and you could use a haircut. You're all shaggy. I can't even see your eyes."

I smile for the first time all day. Mr. Jiang only makes fun of people he likes. He's got a new scraggly beard, like Spock's evil twin in *TOS* episode "Mirror, Mirror." But Mr. Jiang is not evil, nor does he have pointy ears or a full head of hair. I'm starting to get a little bit of fuzz on my upper lip, only it looks like dirt. Ramen has a baby face and if you tell him that he goes ballistic. That's why we all mention it as much as possible.

For a while the AV Club met after school. This is the first year it's an actual class, although now it's called

"Technical Sciences." I think it's great because that means I don't have to take an elective. With my luck, I would have been stuck in Home Studies, where they force you to cook and sew.

"Here's the deal," Mr. Jiang says, lowering his voice. "Even though we're officially Technical Sciences, among us we'll still call ourselves 'the AV Club.'" The entire class, all four of us, break into conspiratorial grins. Ramen and I raise our hands to high-five . . . only we sort of miss and end up doing a high two instead.

AV stands for "audiovisual." The AV Club members are the ones who make sure there's projection, sound, and lighting for all the assemblies and PTA meetings. We're the ones who wheel in the TV sets when teachers want to show a video. We make sure the DVD players run. We can fix a computer and know when it's time to replace a mouse.

AV Club runs the entire freakin' school! Only no one knows it. People think we're geeks. But when something technical goes wrong, who do they turn to? That's right. AV Club. The club consists of me; Ramen; Troy, a fellow Trekker who can pick any lock; and Patrick, who claims that he's the third cousin of Billy Dee Williams, who played Lando Calrissian in the *Star Wars* movies. He wants to be in the next *Star Wars* movie and sends a letter to George Lucas every week.

As Mr. Jiang is telling us about the AV convention he went to in Las Vegas, a new student wanders into the room. He takes a seat in the back, far away from the pod we've formed near the front of the class.

"I'm sorry, I didn't catch your name," Mr. Jiang says.

"Max Cunningham," the kid mumbles.

Mr. Jiang cradles one ear with his hand. "I can't hear you."

"My name is MAX!"

"Ah, that's better. Welcome, Max. Come sit up here with the guys," Mr. Jiang says.

The new kid comes closer, but still sits a row away. He's wearing expensive track shoes with green shoelaces.

"I'm sorry to report that the AV budget got cut again," Mr. Jiang says. "Which means that the new video camera I promised you guys isn't coming this year."

We all moan. Our equipment is so old it's laughable.

"What about the LED board?" Troy asks. He has long-ish wavy blond hair, and from behind he looks like a girl.

"That still may come through," Mr. Jiang tells us. "It was ordered two years ago."

"I'll bet sports haven't been touched," Patrick gripes. He's done his hair in dreadlocks over the summer and if you didn't know him, you might mistake him for one of the cool kids. "Their budgets are never cut."

Mr. Jiang nods as he looks for something on his messy desk. "Priorities can get mixed up."

Don't I know it. In the universe called Rancho Rosetta Middle School, here's our solar system.

In the center is the sun, a large, hot dense mass, a.k.a. the teachers and admin — they're the dictators and they determine the rules. Then in order of importance/closest to the sun you have:

Mercury, the smallest planet — inhabited by popular, good-looking athletes, like Stanford Wong and Dean Hoddin, plus beautiful, scary girls, like Julie

Venus, sister planet to Earth — inhabited by kids who are active in the student body, smart, and liked by teachers

Earth, the most populated planet — inhabited by regular kids: not popular, but not unpopular

Mars, the red planet, dotted with vast volcanoes — inhabited by drama kids, band members, and artsy-fartsy types

Jupiter, whose strong internal heat causes cloud bands — inhabited by slackers and rebels, like skateboarders, bikers, and bullies

Saturn, the least dense planet in the solar system — inhabited by nerds (awkward, smart kids)

Uranus (unfortunate name), which orbits the sun on its side and radiates very little heat — inhabited by geeks (sci-fi/tech kids)

Neptune, cold, dark, and whipped by supersonic
winds — inhabited by dorks (dumb, spazzy kids)
Pluto, which has an eccentric orbit — inhabited by
AV Club (a collection of nerds, dorks, and geeks).
Sadly, Pluto is no longer even considered a planet.

"If Lando were here, he'd get us new equipment," Patrick shouts as he waves his arms in the air. Patrick owns the complete series of *Star Wars* DVDs. What an incredible waste of money. If I had that kind of extra moola, I'd buy a Platinum Pass to the Super *Star Trek* Convention. The platinum one gets you into the ultra-exclusive panels with stars, a special collector's T-shirt, and a guarantee of three to ten autographs.

"Kirk could take down Lando any day," Troy tells him as he shoves a shim into a Master lock and pops it open.

"You're insane!" Patrick barks.

Troy yells back, "You're Jabba the Hut!"

"Yeah, well, you're a Klingon reject!"

Ramen and I jump in and it's *Star Trek* vs. *Star Wars*, full on, full blown. We had this battle every day of AV Club all last year too. Soon, Ramen and Patrick are standing on chairs chanting the catatonic crawl that begins every *Star Wars* movie: "A long time ago / in a galaxy far, far away . . ."

This is more than Troy and I can take. We stand

on chairs facing them and shout in our best William-Shatner-as-Captain-James-T.-Kirk, "Space . . . the Final Frontier . . . TO BOLDLY GO WHERE NO MAN HAS GONE BEFORE."

Mr. Jiang has dozed off. He's heard it all before.

Max takes it all in without saying anything. He looks like a sixth grader. His black hair is short and he's pale and skinny. When the final bell rings Mr. Jiang startles and wakes up. As we all head to the door, Ramen rushes up to Max. "Hey, can I ask you something sort of personal?"

"What?" Max asks.

Ramen doesn't mince words. "*Star Trek* or *Star Wars*?" he says point-blank.

Troy, Patrick, and I hold our breath.

Max doesn't even blink. "Neither," he answers. "Batman."

5.

Batman?

"Batman's a comic book," Ramen cries. He staggers like someone stabbed him in the heart with a rusty screwdriver. "It isn't even sci-fi!"

It's lunchtime the next day, but we're still in shock over the new kid's proclamation. "I know," I moan. "Plus, Batman wears a cape. How stupid is that? A *cape*?"

Ramen's eyes narrow. "Capes are cool. Darth Vader wears one."

"Dorks wear capes," I say, knowing this will throw Ramen into a frenzy.

"Take it back! Take it back!" he screams. "Dorks wear tights like Captain Kirk!"

"Those aren't tights, those are pants! Plus, Captain Kirk could whip Luke Skywalker any day."

"Yeah?" Ramen growls.

"Yeah!" I growl back.

"Clearly there's something wrong with Max," Ramen insists as he resumes eating his noodles with his plastic fork. It's shrimp flavor today. Ramen's so lame that last year he got an Ewok action figure stuck in his nose and had to go to the doctor to have it removed. Still, he does have a point about Max. There's something odd about him, but I can't figure out what it is.

I return to my turkey sandwich. Mom put avocado in it. I love avocados. They're expensive, but one of my mother's golfing buddies has an avocado tree and gives us bags of them for free.

It's already the second week of school. In AV Club Max has proved himself to be an expert in everything. He's starting to get on my nerves, although Mr. Jiang is impressed with him. He even let Max borrow his *AV Pro for the Pro* magazine.

"Max wears a Batman shirt every day," Ramen continues. "How stupid is that?"

Mega stupid, I have to agree again. I wear a *Star Trek* T-shirt every day, and Ramen wears a *Star Wars* one, but that's different. Our shirts make a statement — Max's just look dumb.

"Shut up!" I hiss. "Here he comes."

"Hi, guys," Max says cheerily. "May I join you?"

"Sure," I say, biting into my sandwich.

"Just don't go all Batman on us," Ramen warns.

Max perches on the bench and opens his lunch box. It's one of those padded kinds. He takes out a plastic container filled with sushi and balances it on his lap. Ramen and I are silent as we watch Max methodically mix a foil packet of soy sauce into the lump of green wasabi. Then he picks up a piece of white sushi with his chopsticks and takes a bite, savoring the taste. When he opens his eyes, he notices us staring at him. "What?" he asks. "Haven't you ever seen someone eat yellowtail before?"

Ramen and I glance at each other and smirk. Max is so weird.

As the three of us eat in silence, I hear someone call out, "Hey, Marley, can I talk to you?"

We all look up, surprised — but I'm sure no one is more shocked than me. It's Stanford Wong. Ramen doesn't notice when some noodles slide off his fork and drop on the ground. Max sits up straighter and swallows his sushi. I blink a few times to make sure I'm not seeing an illusion. The popular kids never wander anywhere near the Tragic Tree.

"Marley!" Stanford calls out again. "I need to talk to you."

The last time Stanford Wong and I said more than hello to each other, he betrayed me. It was in elementary school. A few days earlier, I had gone to his house to help him work on his model of *Stargazer* and to admire his 1988 *Star Trek: The Next Generation* Galoob Phaser. He even let me hold it. But the entire time Stanford seemed distant, like he had something other than *Star Trek* on his mind.

Back then I liked all *Star Trek* — any season, any show. Even the *Star Trek* movies. I recall asking Stanford where he got his phaser, and he was all spacey like he didn't hear me. Like I wasn't even there.

The next day he was hanging around the basketball court at recess. He had been doing that more and more — watching the players, studying them. Stanford had even started asking them if he could play. Right. Since when did the somebodies let a nobody into their circle?

"Give up," I told him. "They're never going to let you in." When he didn't say anything, I asked if he wanted to work on our *Star Trek* models after school. One of the basketball players snickered when he heard me mention *Star Trek*.

When Stanford heard him laughing, he turned toward me. He wore an odd look on his face, like he was in pain. "*Star Trek?*" Stanford boomed. "Are you still playing with *Star Trek* stuff? That's only for geeks."

Stunned, all I could think of was to quote *TOS*, Season One, Episode 25: "This is mutiny, mister."

When Stanford turned his back on me, I felt all the blood drain from my face as I began to disappear.

I wince at the memory of that day. Fellow *Star Trek* geek Stanford Wong is long gone. Standing before me is someone I don't know ... star basketball player Stanford Wong. He's my height, only muscular. His hair looks like it has goop in it and the tips are purple. The basketball shoes he's wearing look complicated and expensive. From the way he's standing, with one hand on his hip, it's painfully clear that he's not from my planet.

"What do you want?" I ask. I wonder if this has anything to do with the Vulcan salute he gave me at the Hee-Haw Game.

Stanford looks at Max and Ramen. Both just gawk at him with their mouths hanging open. I've seen people look at him that way — like he's some big shot, when really he's a jerk.

"Uh, Marley, can I talk to you?" the jerk asks again. "Alone?"

"I guess," I say as we move away from the bench. I can feel Ramen's and Max's eyes following us.

Stanford is holding a basketball. He always carries one around school, probably to telegraph, "I am a jock and you should bow to me." There's an awkward silence. Finally, he says, "You still into *Star Trek*?"

I nod. What a stupid question. I'm wearing my VUL-CANS RULE T-shirt. I don't tell him that I have a plastic figure of Sulu in my pocket. "What about you?" I ask.

Stanford shakes his head. "No. Not so much. Maybe a little. Hey, I wanted to give you —"

"HEY, STANFORD!" someone yells. It's Gus, one of

his basketball buddies. I had Honors English with him last year and he drove Mr. Glick crazy with his questions. "Come on! We gotta go!"

The rest of Stanford's gang is standing around waiting for him. There's Tico — he's never been mean to me — and Stretch, the best-looking kid at our school, and probably any school in America.

"We're waiting!" Gus shouts.

Stanford looks distracted. "I . . . um, do you hate me?"

That's a weird question for him to ask. Should I lie or tell the truth?

"I guess so," I say.

His shoulders slump. "Never mind, then. I gotta go."

"Then go," I tell him. But he's already gone.

What was that all about?

I watch Stanford Wong rejoin the planet of the popular kids, then I return to the broken bench, and the Tragic Tree, and Ramen and Max.

"What did he want?" Ramen asks.

"Was that Stanford Wong?" Max says. "Isn't he a legend around here or something?"

"What did he want?" Ramen asks again.

"Nothing."

"He came all the way over here for nothing?" Ramen asks.

I nod and take a bite of my sandwich even though I'm not hungry.

6.

Horrible sounds are assaulting me as I make my way down the narrow staircase. The closer I get, the worse it is. I cover the rubber Spock ears I'm wearing and peer into one of the rooms beneath the Rialto stage. I see a little kid, her feet dangling from the piano bench, pounding the piano keys.

"I'm home!" I yell above the noise.

Mom smiles, then turns to the little girl in pink overalls. "That's great, Kylie. Now let's try it again. This time I want you to wiggle your fingers in the air to relax them before you start."

My mother's a piano teacher. She's also the organist for the Rialto. Every now and then Dad will run silent movies, and Mom will play the ancient Wurlitzer. It's a really big, beautiful organ with rows of glistening keys. I like to imagine it soaring through space like the *Enterprise*, and leaving a trail of musical notes in its wake.

Dad doesn't call the Rialto a movie theater; he calls it a movie palace. He takes the tickets, keeps the concession stand stocked, runs the projector, cleans up — pretty much everything. My family owns the place. Our upstairs apartment is tiny, but I have the run of the theater when there are no movies playing. In its heyday it seated 1,200. Nowadays, if there are twelve people per show, Dad's happy.

This theater is nothing like those sterile mall multiplexes with their endless row of ticket booths stuffed with bored high schoolers who wouldn't know a cinematic classic if they saw one. The Rialto's beautiful, from the red velvet curtains to the statues of gargoyles. Fancy lights line the theater walls and hand-painted clouds and angels are on the ceiling. Even the bathrooms have shiny gold faucets. I know. I'm in charge of cleaning them.

Every now and then, there will be a television special or magazine article about old theaters and the Rialto will be featured. For a couple weeks after, we'll have lots of business. But gradually the lines thin and it's back to the regulars — mostly movie buffs or the occasional man trying to impress his date with his knowledge of films.

My favorite part of the theater is someplace few people have seen. Down in the basement are huge steamer trunks filled with vintage costumes and crazy props, like cow bells, top hats, and fake flowers, from the Rialto's heyday, when it was a vaudeville theater. If you're quiet you can almost hear the hubbub of the performers between acts.

Ramen swears the Rialto is haunted and gets all weirded out whenever he comes over, just because legend has it that a ghost lives in the theater. Stanford Wong used to come here all the time. The ghost rumors never fazed him. Stanford always claimed he wanted to come face-to-face with the ghost.

Some say that the ghost is a man who committed suicide in the projection booth after watching *Un Chien Andalou* for five straight days. It's a really bizarre old movie that has a giant eyeball in it. If I had to watch it for five days straight I'd kill myself. Still, there are other movies that I don't mind seeing over and over again, like the original *King Kong* and *Miracle on 34th Street*. I also like *The Red Badge of Courage*, about a Civil War soldier who tries to find the nerve to fight in battle.

Today Ms. McKenna told us that we have an American history test coming up. Well, she didn't so much tell us, as she did a rap . . .

> *History is great*
> *But don't you wait.*
> *Start to study now*
> *And don't have a cow.*
> *Sha boom! Sha boom!*
> *Crack open your books*

Or you'll get bad looks
When you take the test
And don't do your best.
Sha boom! Sha boom!

There was stunned silence in the classroom when she was done.

I can still hear my mom's student torturing the piano as I head downstairs to do my homework. I yank on a chain and the light from a bare bulb floods the basement. I've put the vaudeville props and costumes on one side of the room and the musical instruments under the stairs. Leaning against one wall are boxes filled with stuff people left behind. There are five pocket watches (one still works), an embroidered handkerchief, and a fancy silver cigarette case with the inscription TO MY LOVE, MAY YOU KEEP THIS ALWAYS.

Over in the corner is the trunk filled with the American Revolution costumes. As I dig through the clothes I discover a plain, long, brown velvet jacket with gold buttons. It looks exactly like something Benjamin Franklin might have worn.

I slip my arm into the costume. It fits! I'm not sure that the jacket matches my Vulcan ears, but it feels right, especially when I put on a pair of old-fashioned glasses. I crack open my American history book. Last year Dad showed

Johnny Tremain, a movie about a patriot who fights to free the colonies from England. It was on a double bill with D. W. Griffith's American Revolution silent film *The Hessian Renegades*. Only a couple people came to see it, but I thought both were great. I can already tell I'll ace McKenna's history class.

On my way home from school today, I stopped at Stahl Miller, the stationery store on Mission Street, and bought something. I open the bag and take out a small black leather-bound notebook. The spine cracks when I open to the first page.

CAPTAIN'S LOG

Original Captain's Log remains missing. Classified information may have been compromised. Today marks the first entry in replacement log book.

I hate P.E. Whoever invented it was evil. Pure evil.

We're picking teams for softball. It's down to that weird guy with thick glasses who always says "wassup," a girl with a limp, and me. Even though I am standing perfectly still, my heart is racing. I glance at the team captains. Neither looks pleased. In fact, both look disgusted.

"You, with the glasses," one of the team captains says as he motions to the boy next to me. The kid releases a little whimper of relief.

The other team captain studies the girl with the limp, and me. She shakes her head as she points to the girl.

The two teams head toward the softball field. I am left standing alone.

"Go," Coach Martin says to me. "You're on that

team." I jog up to the boy with the glasses who's lagging behind. Neither of us says anything. We don't have to.

Even though I was picked last, I am the first one to strike out. The only thing worse than everyone ignoring me is everyone glaring at me.

"Sports are stupid," Ramen says at lunch. "I can't catch the ball and I throw like a girl."

"Don't insult the girls," Max chimes in, adding, "dodgeball's the worst. I mean, they form a circle so no one can escape and then hurl balls at you? This is a school-sanctioned activity — and you're graded on it?"

We all break out laughing. Max is okay. A Frisbee lands at our feet. All three of us stare at it like it's a flaming-hot meteor. Some skater kid with helmet hair and a deep voice calls out, "Hey! Throw it over here." None of us move. "Guys," he yells impatiently as he holds his hands up in the air, "the Frisbee!"

I bend down and pick it up. Then I walk it over and hand it to him. "Thanks," he says, giving me the once-over. "But you could have just thrown it."

That's not true. I can't throw a Frisbee. I can't catch a ball or do a dozen push-ups without getting winded. I can't kick a soccer ball or climb a rope. But I can recite every *Star Trek* episode title by year, even naming the guest stars. Why don't we ever do that in P.E.?

"I'm building a model of the Batmobile from scratch," Max informs me when I return. He's eating a salad today. I have a peanut butter sandwich on Mom's homemade sourdough bread. "It's going to be remote controlled," he continues. "I got everything I need at RadioShack. Plus, I have a couple of mini Batman action figures that fit perfectly. You should see the Riddler. He's totally awesome."

Ramen and I look at each other and try not to yawn. Max is wearing a red Batman shirt with the Joker on it. He wears his T-shirts tucked into his jeans and even I know it looks weird.

"Hey, Max." I take a swig from my water bottle. "Just a couple of pointers. First, you should never wear a red shirt. In the original *Star Trek* series, the security guys wore red shirts and usually at least one of them would end up dead before the episode ended. So basically, red shirts equal death. And second, I'm not sure where you come from, but around here, guys never tuck in their T-shirts."

"Why are you telling me this?" Max asks, throwing me a hard glare.

"Because red gives off bad karma. I just thought you'd want to know."

"Not that!" Max sounds agitated. "Why did you tell me that guys never tuck in their shirts?"

Ramen steps in. "People already think AV Club guys are geeks, so if you keep tucking in your shirt, that'll make you a double geek, 'cause it makes you look like a girl."

Max's cheeks flush bright red. He clenches his fists and glares at Ramen, then me. The force of his anger causes us both to take a step backward. "Is that what you think?" Max yells. "Is that what you think? That I look like a girl?"

"Well, I'm just saying," Ramen mumbles, "that if you keep it up you could be mistaken for one."

I nod.

Max shoves Ramen so hard that he hits the Tragic Tree and falls down in the mud. Before I can react, Max comes toward me with his fists clenched. I step back, but he's in my face. "For your information, you dweebs," Max yells, "I AM A GIRL!"

"You're . . . you're . . . you're a girl?" I stammer. When Max's face contorts, I quickly say, "Of course you're a girl. We knew that."

I turn to Ramen for backup, but he's just sitting in the mud with his mouth hanging open.

Max isn't moving.

Neither am I.

I am about to turn away when I notice Max's eyes filling with tears. I open my mouth to speak, but before any words come out, Max shoves me to the ground, then runs away. Now that I'm paying attention, I notice that he . . . *she* does run like a girl.

As Ramen and I sit in the mud, he turns to me and says, "Who knew?"

I shake my head. "Not me," I answer. "Not me."

CAPTAIN'S LOG

Major miscalculation of new crew member's origins.

8.

Max completely ignored Ramen and me the rest of the day. Everyone else does, so why not Max now too? The only difference is that most people don't even realize they're ignoring us. Max actually made an effort. Not that I blame her.

"I'm confused," says Ramen as we leave AV Club. Today Mr. Jiang led a heated debate about pixels and Max didn't even chime in once.

"I know. I could have sworn she was a he," I say. My backpack feels heavier than usual. I weighed it once and was told that it was 17.5 pounds and had no body fat. (I had put it on my mom's talking scale.)

"I'm confused," Ramen says again.

"You've always been confused," I assure him as I remove the rock someone put in my backpack. "Like that *Star Wars* is better than *Star Trek*! Wookiee, Wookiee, Wookiee," I sing. "Wookiee, Wookiee!"

He starts shoving me back and we're laughing and pushing each other in the hallway and yelling "Wookiee!" and "Klingon!"

"Look," I tell Ramen, "Max is over there. Let's talk to her." As we head in her direction, she slams her locker shut and scurries away. "Hey, Max!" I shout as she ducks behind some kids in the crowded hallway. "Wait up!"

Suddenly, *BOOM!* I'm on the ground and so is someone else. "Hey, sorry," I stutter as I start to get up.

"Sorry is not enough," Digger says as he rises. His eyes narrow as he looks me over. "What's your name?"

I've had classes with Digger for years and he still doesn't know my name?

"What's your name?" he repeats. His goons are standing nearby smirking. They're wearing Roadrunner jackets. Didn't Stanford used to be a Roadrunner?

"My name's . . . Victor Lazlo," I tell him.

"Victor," Digger says, "you'd better not cross me again. I'll be watching you."

Ramen and I don't move as he walks away. We're like two frozen Borg in the Arctic. Finally, when Digger is out of sight, Ramen asks, "Who's Victor Lazlo?"

"Just someone from the movies," I say.

Ramen shakes his head. "Oh man, it was nice knowing you, Victor."

"Stop it," I say. My knees feel weak.

"Digger's gonna kill you. He's gonna kill you, and if he doesn't kill you he's going to make sure you suffer for the rest of your life."

"Ramen —"

"Yeah?"

"Shut up."

"Digger's gonna kill you," Ramen whispers again. "And it isn't going to be pretty. Hey! If he does kill you, can I have your backpack? Mine's got a hole in it."

The next day, all through history, as Ms. McKenna waves her arms and talks about the American Revolution, Digger stares at me as if daring me to look him in the eyes. I can feel the heat of his glare.

". . . so that's what we will cover on the quiz next week," Ms. McKenna says. She's wearing a lot of bracelets, which have been jangling practically nonstop. "Now I have an important question." She waits until she has everyone's attention, which takes a long time, then asks, "Who has the most songs on their MP3 player?"

Several kids raise their hands. Ms. McKenna turns on her ancient boom box and starts dancing to some idiot song. "Everyone join me!" She's now attempting to do the moonwalk, but only succeeding in looking like she's trying to smush a bug. Everyone remains rooted in their chairs, clearly stunned. Her attempt at being cool is pitiful. The only thing more pitiful than her is me.

It's one thing to get punched in the arm by the Gorn, but a completely different thing to be marked for death by Digger.

I imagine my funeral. It's tragic, but nice. My father is sitting in the front row of the Rialto weeping as my mother plays the Wurlitzer. Mr. Jiang is taking a nap. Ramen is wearing my backpack and eating noodles. Troy is picking a lock and Patrick's playing *Star Wars* on his DS, as Ms. McKenna is dancing, oblivious to how dumb she looks.

CAPTAIN'S LOG

Powerful enemy on the horizon. Activate protective force field.

9.

Max glowers at me when I enter AV Club the next day. I sit far away from him — *her*. I sit far away from her. This is going to take some getting used to.

"Our new LED board should arrive tomorrow," Mr. Jiang says excitedly. "Anyone familiar with LED boards?"

Max raises her hand. She's become Mr. Jiang's favorite, just because when the PA system went down during another boring speech by Principal Haycorn, Max was able to fix it. Big deal. If I had brought my action figure of Scotty, the USS *Enterprise*'s chief engineer, I could have fixed it too.

Patrick is chomping on barbecue CornNuts. The noise sounds like a jackhammer and reminds me of the *Star Trek: Deep Space Nine* episode "Chrysalis" where three genetically enhanced humans conclude that the earth will collapse on itself in a "Big Crunch."

"Hey," I whisper to Patrick. He stops chewing. "Did you know that Max is a girl?"

He nods and offers me a CornNut.

"Troy," I say as I crunch. "Did you know that Max is a girl?"

He nods.

How is it that only Ramen and I didn't know? Maybe it's 'cause we don't hang around girls very much. Or rather, they don't hang around us. Actually, nobody hangs out with us. Ramen and I had been eating lunch, just the two of us, for years until Max showed up.

I peer at Max. She's wearing purple shoelaces. How could I have been so dumb?

Mr. Jiang is going over the list of what classes are going to need AV equipment delivered tomorrow. The way it works is that we rotate AV setup and delivery sixth period, and if a teacher needs something during another period and any of us are in P.E., we can skip it to provide AV assistance. I always pray someone will show a movie when I have P.E.

There's a PTA meeting next week. Max volunteers to man it. "They'll need a mike and a TV and DVD player," Mr. Jiang is saying as he settles into his worn swivel chair. There are bumper stickers all over the back of it, including one that reads ZERO TO WARP 9.7 IN 3 SECONDS. Another one says DROIDS WELCOMED HERE, and recently a BATMAN FOREVER sticker materialized.

"Okay, now, Ramen and Marley, you two sort through our extension cords," Mr. Jiang orders. "Some of them are really frayed, and if they cause a fire and burn down the school, it would be catastrophic because I'll be out of a job. The rest of you, clean the AV carts."

"Should we say something to her?" Ramen whispers as he sneaks a peek at Max. He tosses a chewed-up extension cord into the reject pile. "We should apologize. Come on."

Max is tightening the wheel bolts on one of the carts. "Yo," Ramen calls out as he saunters over to her. "Yo, mama!" I roll my eyes. Max looks up. Her face is blank as he says, "There's something that Marley wants to tell you —"

Huh?

Max blinks at me, still stone-faced. "What?"

"Well," I begin. "We knew you weren't a boy —"

"Liar," Max snaps.

I don't like the way she's gripping the wrench.

I start over. "Um, hey, we're really sorry. It's just that, well, you were so good at AV stuff it never occurred to us that you could be a girl."

Max just stares at me with her arms crossed.

"I didn't mean it like that." I try to backtrack. "What I meant was that most girls are all girly and stuff, and you're not. And girls don't know the first thing about AV equipment since a girl wouldn't be caught dead in AV Club —"

Max cuts me off. "Marley! You'd better stop before you get both feet stuck in your mouth." She yells across the room to Mr. Jiang, "This AV cart is ready to go!"

"Great," he answers as he thumbs through his *Electronics Today* magazine. "Deliver it to room 27, and be sure to take a hall pass."

After Max leaves, I glare at Ramen. He's such an idiot. "Why didn't you back me up? The apology was supposed to be from both of us."

"I wasn't about to put myself in front of your train wreck." He takes a container of Mega-Mini-Mints out of his pocket and pours them into his mouth.

"You're the one who said we should apologize!" I remind him.

"Nooooo, it was you!" Ramen insists. A couple of Mini-Mints fly out of his mouth when he yells and one hits me in the face. "You were the one who was all weirded out to find out Max was a girl."

"You were even more surprised than I was!"

"Was not!"

"Was so!"

"Was not!

"Was so!"

There's only one way to settle this. Our eyes narrow as Ramen and I brace for the inevitable. We both nod in unison, shake our fists at each other, and chant, "Laser! Taser! Phaser! Go!"

"Ha!" I call out. "Scissors beats paper, I win!"

For years we've been trying to think of hand signals for a laser, taser, and phaser, and arguing what would trump the other. But since we can't agree, we substitute rock, paper, scissors when the challenge actually begins.

I love playing Laser, Taser, Phaser with Ramen because he's such a sore loser. Max was good at Laser, Taser, Phaser even though we had just taught her. It was sort of cool hanging out with someone who wasn't Ramen, even if Max is delusional and thinks that Batman actually matters.

As Ramen grumbles about a rematch, I wonder if Max is ever going to eat lunch with us again.

I hope she does.

When I get home, my father is balancing on the wobbly wooden ladder. I wish he'd get one that's not held together with duct tape. He's changing the Rialto marquee to read TO KILL A MOCKINGBIRD. I love that movie. Dad sort of looks like Gregory Peck, the actor who plays Atticus Finch, except that my father doesn't wear glasses or own a suit. Also Dad's hair is light brown like mine, but he's as tall as Gregory Peck and I get my height from him.

When my father's happy, two deep dimples appear near his smile. My mother loves this about him. He also has a scar about the size of a small paper clip below his left eye. I've asked him about it many times. He never gives me a straight answer, instead saying, "I got it when I wrestled a mountain lion." Or, "It's just an old war wound." Or, "Klingon, Marley. The Klingon left me this as a gift."

My father climbs down the ladder and retrieves a wrinkled piece of paper from his pocket. "Your mom needs these things from the grocery store. You mind getting them?"

"If I do it, can I get Doritos?"

"Only if you share," he quips. Mom doesn't approve of junk food. She's got a thing about eating healthy.

"It's a deal," I tell my father. He doesn't like to go out if he can help it. Usually my mother does the grocery shopping, but she's at her yoga lesson at the YMCA. Mom also takes spinning classes there. That's where people pedal bikes to nowhere.

I call Dial-a-Ride and wait outside for the van. Technically, it's for senior citizens and people who are handicapped. But Cedra, the driver, doesn't get a lot of calls, so usually she's happy to drive my father and me around too. In exchange, Dad lets her into the Rialto for free, and gives her unlimited popcorn. Cedra's really nice, even if she does look scary. She has a blue Mohawk and her entire left arm is covered with tattoos. Her nose and lip are pierced. Plus, she drives superfast, like warp-speed fast.

I glance at my mom's grocery list. It's typed as always. You should see how fast she types. I'm surprised the keyboard doesn't catch on fire. I installed a TWP for her — a talking word processor. Mr. Jiang helped me pick it out. It can read aloud each letter or word as she types. But Mom hardly ever uses it. "Why should I?" she says. "I already know what I wrote."

I remember when I was learning to type, I'd get so

frustrated. "Put your fingers on the keyboard," my mother instructed. "Now, Marley, can you see the letter F and the letter J? Rest your index fingers on both those keys." I did what she told me. "What do you feel?"

"There are little bumps on them," I said, surprised.

"That's so you can always be sure your fingers are in the right position, even if you're not looking — or happen to be blind!"

Mom's been blind as long as I can remember. She wasn't always, though. When she was a girl, she could see, and then she got retinitis pigmentosa, an eye disease, and slowly she started losing her sight. My mother makes me go to the eye doctor once a year, just to make sure it won't happen to me.

Cedra pulls up and puts out her cigarette when I jump in. "Bridge Market," I tell her. They let us buy groceries on credit there.

I get everything on the list, plus Doritos. It looks like Mom's going to make her famous white bean and chicken chili. While I wait for Cedra to come back, I sit on a bench and stuff my face with the chips. They turn my fingers orange, but I don't care. It's worth it. As I'm crunching, I spy Max across the street, looking in the window of Van Straaten's Sports Closet. There are a bunch of girls near her, but you can tell she's not with them. Julie is pointing at Max. Then all the other girls laugh. As Max walks away with her shoulders hunched, I want to go over to her so she won't be by herself. I know how it feels to be made fun of. But I've got all these grocery bags, and Cedra's coming soon, and maybe Max won't want to talk to me, and . . .

A horn honks. Cedra's here. I guess I shouldn't keep her waiting.

I put the groceries on the kitchen counter. Mom comes in and stops cold. "I'm disappointed," she says. "Doritos."

Never underestimate my mother's sense of smell.

"Sorry," I say. "It's just that they were calling my name. Marleeeey, Marleeeeey . . ."

Mom laughs. "Okay, Marleeeeey, in exchange for your junk food folly, you will accompany me to the driving range tonight. After your homework, of course."

"Yes, Mother," I say, pretending to moan. We both know that I'd go with her to the driving range — Doritos or no Doritos.

I head to my room and take my Sulu action figure out of my pocket. It looks like his hand is about to fall off. I should be more careful. Without hands, Sulu wouldn't be able to steer the *Enterprise*.

I open my backpack. Why are the teachers piling so much homework on us? They're trying to kill us, aren't they? My desk is really small and my model of the *Enterprise* takes up most of it. I'm almost done with it. From my window I catch sight of a group of boys heading down the street. They take up the entire sidewalk, like they own it. It's Stanford and his friends. To make sure they don't see me, I grab my homework, slip on my Spock ears, and sit on the floor to finish it. The math's easy and I whip through it. In English we have to write an essay about our family. The assignment isn't due for a while, so there's no point in doing it now, since I could get killed by an asteroid, or Digger, tomorrow.

It's been a while since Stanford walked by. All I have left for homework is history. I stand and stretch, then head to the basement. "Dinner in one hour," Mom calls out.

I yank on the storage room light and slip on the Benjamin Franklin jacket. It feels right to be wearing this, like I've used the *Star Trek* transporter to journey to another place and time. In *TOS*, "The City on the Edge of Forever," the *Star Trek* crew was able to observe parts of the American Revolution through a time portal. I would give anything to be in another place and time.

I pop out the lenses of the Ben Franklin glasses and put them on too. As I read my history book aloud, I lower my voice and stride across the room and wave my hand in the air to punctuate the important parts. I read ahead even though Ms. McKenna hasn't assigned it yet. History is so fascinating — the battles, the intrigue, the double crosses. Now that I think about it, it's sort of like *Star Trek*.

When I'm done, I forage through the old offices that line one hallway. There are little rooms and alcoves everywhere. It takes a long time, but I push a huge, old metal desk down the hall and into the storage room. Even though it's rusted, some of the drawers still open. In the corner of an abandoned dressing room I find a red velvet throne. That'll make a fine captain's chair. I spend the rest of the afternoon setting up my space. There's a fancy lamp — it's broken, but I rewire it, and the wooden coat tree is perfect for hanging my Ben Franklin jacket. "A place for everything, and everything in its place," Benjamin Franklin once said.

Finally, I go upstairs and bring down most of my *Star Trek* action figures. I line them up in order of their first appearance on the TV series and movies. Then I stand back and survey what I have created. I smile. I am no longer in the basement of the Rialto.

CAPTAIN'S LOG

Reconfigured unused area of space station's lower deck into facsimile of USS Enterprise to include the Bridge and Transporter Room. Only authorized personnel may enter.

11.

There was a *Star Trek* marathon on television over the weekend, so you know where I was. Now it's Monday morning. Dad's sleeping in. The Rialto is dark on Mondays and it's his only day off. Mom's doing yoga as she listens to one of her audiobooks. This one's about the green rolling hills of Tuscany. Her dream is to visit Italy and ride a gondola with Dad. But I doubt that's ever going to happen. She can barely get my father out of the Rialto for a walk in the park.

"Have a great day, Marley," Mom calls out. She looks like a pretzel. "Wait, aren't you forgetting something?"

I turn around and give her a hug. Hugs are her thing.

As I wait on the corner for the light to change color, someone sneaks up from behind and hisses in my ear, "Hello, Victor."

My heart drops into my stomach. Digger is standing next to me. He's wearing a sinister smile. The light turns green, but I can't move. "Aren't you going to say hello to me, Victor?" Digger asks politely.

It takes me a moment to realize he's talking to me. I shut my eyes, hoping to be beamed up and out of here. When I open them, Digger is staring at me.

"Victor, didn't you hear me? I asked if you did your history homework."

I nod. Why is Digger trying to make small talk with me?

"Let me see it," he orders.

"Excuse me?"

His blue eyes flash. "You seem to be having trouble hearing. I said, let me see it."

We're in public, in broad daylight. So why am I so nervous? I'm taller than him, but Digger is solid and he's just plain scary. He's scarier than the Salt Vampire from *TOS*, "The Man Trap," or even Gul Dukat in *Star Trek: Deep Space Nine*. Rumor has it that Digger once got a teacher fired. Even the most evil *Star Trek* villains didn't have the power to do that.

I rummage through my backpack and hand over my homework.

"Who's 'Marley Sandski'?" Digger asks as he looks at it. His Roadrunners jacket has DIGGER RONSTER embroidered on it in fancy lettering.

"San-del-ski. That's my name," I croak. The light's

turned green twice since we've been standing here, not that I'm counting.

"I guess it doesn't matter whose it is," Digger tells me as he shoves my homework into his backpack. "It's mine now anyway. Thanks, Victor Lazlo, or Marley San-del-ski, or whoever you are."

The light turns green again. He strolls across the street and leaves me standing on the corner.

"... and so," Ms. McKenna tells us, "the revolution was revolutionary!" She takes a tissue from the box on her desk and wipes a tear off her cheek. "Don't all of you just love, love, love history?" When no one answers, she clears her throat and says. "Well, then. Homework, please."

At the end of class, Ms. McKenna comes up to me as I am getting ready to leave. "Marley," she says. She's wearing her red Converse again. "I don't have your homework. Where is it?"

"I don't know," I mumble.

"Did you do it?"

"Yes."

"Then please hand it in," she says.

"I can't."

"I see." Her eyes darken. The room is empty now. Ms. McKenna asks, "Do you want to tell me where your homework is?"

"Not really," I say. I'm looking at the floor. I wear Converse too. Black high-tops. Well, not really Converse, but a knockoff of them. The real ones cost too —

"Mr. Sandelski?"

"Huh?" I think it sounds so stupid when teachers call us Mr. and Ms. Whatever. Like they're trying to make whatever they have to say sound more important than it really is.

"You can hand it in tomorrow, Mr. Sandelski," she says. "But don't do this again."

"Yes, ma'am. May I be excused? I don't want to be late to Technical Sciences."

Ms. McKenna lets out a tired sigh. "Go on, then. Don't be late."

As I leave the room, I almost crash into Stanford Wong and two of his basketball buddies. They are commanding the center of the hallway. Everyone steps aside as they come through. "Hi, Stanford!" echoes down the corridor.

Stanford's friend Stretch doesn't say hello to anyone. Unlike Stanford, who looks like he's lapping up all the attention, Stretch appears to be in pain every time someone says something to him. Then there's Tico. He's one of the rare popular kids who's nice to everyone, even nobodies. One time, when Ramen was at the library, someone tied his shoelaces together. When he stood up and tried to walk, he fell. Everyone laughed, except for Tico, who helped him up.

I spot Max. Along with everyone else, she's staring at Stretch. Max hasn't spoken to me all week.

I slip into Mr. Jiang's class just as the bell rings. Patrick is testing the projector. Troy is picking a lock with a paper clip. Picking locks is much easier than you'd imagine. Sometimes Troy gives us lessons.

"Are you going to use your skills for good or evil?" Ramen asks.

Troy looks insulted. "For good," he says. "I'm going to be an Interpol spy."

Ramen leaves to deliver a television to Mr. Glick's English class. Max is trying to get the LED message board out of the box. I go over to help her. Without saying a word we manage to unwrap it. She's wearing a Batman/*Dark Knight* shirt with Christian Bale on it. It looks new.

Mr. Jiang bounds over. "Let's hope this one works better than the last one they sent!"

Max is already plugging it in. "It only uses fifteen watts of power," she says. "Plus, it's got a three-color LED. The wide-viewing angle will make it easy to read from across the cafeteria."

"Does it have antiglare?" I ask.

"Well, duh, yes," she says dismissively. "It's state of the art . . . or did you not notice that?"

Max is already programming the board via a remote keyboard. From what I can see, there's a single Ethernet connection.

"Marley, hit the light switch," she orders. I do as I am told. "Three, two, one —" Max presses a button and the board lights up. On the screen is a scroll that reads MAR-LEY SANDELSKI IS A LOSER . . . LOSER . . . LOSER . . .

I take one look at my name in bright red lights and my throat tightens. It's one thing to hear it, but another to see it like it's official.

I need some fresh air.

As I am pacing in the hallway, I hear Principal Haycorn call out, "Young man, where is your hall pass?"

Great. I'm in real trouble now.

CAPTAIN'S LOG

Ambushed in plain sight. Need to discern friends from foes.

My parents are whispering about money again. Or rather, they are whispering about our lack of it. When I get older, I'm going to be rich and give them bags of money so they don't have to worry anymore.

"I made some scrambled eggs with cheese and scallions, the way you like it," my mother says as I set the table for breakfast.

It's a good thing my mother loves to cook. Dad says he'd rather eat her food than at a restaurant any day. Every now and then Mom and I treat ourselves to Stout's Coffee Shop. Libby, the waitress with the poufy hair, is always really nice to both of us. Even though we don't go there very often, she remembers that I like extra whipped cream on my hot chocolate, and that my mother likes her coffee with cream and two sugars, and that we both love the homemade French silk pie with those curls of chocolate on the top. We always bring a slice home for Dad.

"Where were you yesterday? I didn't see you in AV Club when I got back."

Ramen is hovering as I try to clean my locker before first period. Someone wrote GEEK on it again. I keep a rag and a bottle of Windex in my locker for situations like this. "Principal's office," I say as I scrub.

"No way!" Ramen looks impressed. "What for? Did you steal something? Did you get in a fight? Oh my God, you killed someone, didn't you? Who was it? Was it Dean Hoddin? It was Coach Martin, wasn't it? You can tell me, I can keep a secret —"

"I didn't have a hall pass."

I've only managed to get part of the word off my locker, so now it reads EEK.

"Is that all?" Ramen looks deflated. He picks at a hole in his *Star Wars* shirt, making it worse. "So what did Haycorn do to you?"

"I had to sit in the office until school got out, but that was less then ten minutes. Then he pointed his fat finger at me and said, 'I never forget a face. I'm going to keep an eye on you!'"

"Well, wandering the halls without a pass was very Han Solo," Ramen notes. He's always bragging about the rebel things he's going to do, yet he always uses the crosswalks and turns his library books in two days early. He was a safety monitor in elementary school.

We head to homeroom. I've redone my history assignment, so I set it on Ms. McKenna's desk next to her pencil holder shaped like a cowboy boot. Ramen follows me to my seat. "You missed seeing what Max can do with the LED message board."

"Oh, I've seen what she can do, all right."

"Yeah!" Ramen says, his voice rising. "She's figured out graphics and animated scrolls and everything!"

"Did you read what it said?" I ask, wondering if the whole AV Club saw the immortal words, "Marley Sandelski is a loser."

"Max programmed it to say 'Go Tiggy' and then there was this really cool animated tiger jumping all around."

"Was there anything else?"

"Naw, but that was really impressive. She's not so bad for a girl. I even told her so."

"What did she say?"

"She said I was a sexist ignoramus who needed a brain transplant. Max is kinda sensitive, don't you think?"

"She's a girl," I remind him.

Other than being thrown in the gym shower with all my clothes on, and trying to avoid eye contact with Digger in Ms. McKenna's class, it's a regular day. Ramen eats his noodles. I get punched by the Gorn.

Thank God for sixth period.

Whenever one of us walks into AV Club, the other members shout hello or yell out some insult, but not the mean kind like the kids in the hallway. Out of a school of 600 students, I can count on three of them acknowledging me. It used to be four until Max got all mad.

It's not that I want to be popular, like Stanford Wong–popular, it's just that I don't want to be unpopular. Sure, popular kids eat at the best tables in the cafeteria, and win all the sports awards, and as a rule look better than the general population. But I'd settle for never getting beat up by the Gorn, or no longer being spit on, or having my locker graffiti-free for just one month. Heck, I'd take one week. And if just a few kids could be nice to me, then maybe school would be less like a battlefield.

Mr. Jiang is sitting at his desk with his feet up. He's wearing mismatched socks again. His head is tilted back as he pours the remains from the bottom of a bag of BBQ chips into his mouth. Some crumbs lodge in his beard. The guys are arguing over which one of us would make the best superhero.

"Me, of course," Troy announces. He's wearing a really cool *Star Trek* shirt with Chris Pine as young Kirk on it. "You have to be smart to be a superhero," Troy is saying, "and that's me."

"Right. You smart? You're as smart as snot," Patrick scoffs. On his shirt, under a picture of Darth Vader, are the words WHO'S YOUR DADDY? "Hey, what did Kirk leave in the toilet?" Troy and I shake our heads. We've heard this joke a million times. "His Captain's log!" Patrick shouts and then high-fives Ramen. "Anyway, I'd be the best superhero since I'm both smart and good-looking!"

"Sorry, guys, it's me," I tell them. "Smart, good-looking, and brave!"

As everyone cracks up, I steal a sideways glance at Max. She's in the back working on the projector. Either she can't hear us, or she's really good at faking it.

"You're all wrong," Ramen tells us. "I am the one and only true superhero of Rancho Rosetta Middle School and to prove it —"

Just then, Mr. Jiang screams and falls out of his chair. Instantly, Max sprints over. "Mr. Jiang, can you hear me?" she shouts.

Mr. Jiang nods. He's curled up on the floor. His face is contorted like he's in a lot of pain. "It . . . it hurts," he groans.

Max looks up and barks, "Patrick, call the main office on the room phone. Troy, run to the office in case Patrick can't get through. Marley, Ramen, clear a path from the door to Mr. Jiang for when help comes." When we all remain frozen, Max shouts, "NOW! DO IT NOW!"

Troy takes off running and Patrick picks up the room phone and starts punching the numbers. Ramen and I start moving AV equipment and tables. Mr. Jiang is still moaning. "It's going to be all right," Max assures him. "We're getting help." She flips open her cell phone and dials.

"You're not supposed to use your cell phone during school," Ramen cautions her.

Max glares at him with such defiance that he slaps both hands over his mouth.

"I'm fine," Mr. Jiang gasps. He's pale.

"You look awful," Ramen tells him.

"Help is on the way, Mr. Jiang," Max says. "Just focus on breathing." Her voice is calm. How can she stay so calm? My heart is racing and I feel helpless.

Suddenly, Principal Haycorn and the school nurse burst through the door. Patrick puts down the room phone. "I was trying to call you," he explains. "But I didn't know the number."

Max, Ramen, and I step aside so the adults can get to Mr. Jiang. The nurse takes one look at him and says to Principal Haycorn, "Call 9-1-1. He needs to be in a hospital."

Max steps up. "I've already called 9-1-1, they're on their way." She looks at me. "Marley, go outside in front of the school so you can direct them to this classroom."

I take off running. Just as I get to the sidewalk, the ambulance shows up with the sirens on. The paramedics grab a stretcher and follow me as I race back to Mr. Jiang's room. The AV Club guys stay out of their way as Mr. Jiang is carried out. Then we follow the paramedics outside and watch helplessly as the ambulance roars away with our teacher inside.

CAPTAIN'S LOG

Comrade down. Diagnosis unknown.

13.

I couldn't sleep all night, I was so worried about Mr. Jiang. What if he's dying? What if he's dead? I've never known anyone who had to ride in an ambulance before. Mom tried calling the hospital, but they wouldn't give out any information.

I skip breakfast and head directly to Principal Haycorn's office. Max is already there. Troy, Patrick, and Ramen all arrive at the same time.

"He's going to be just fine," Principal Haycorn assures us as he adjusts his bow tie in the mirror behind his door. There's a terrible smell in his office and I try not to gag. That's when I spot a bottle of Mantique cologne on his bookshelf. "His appendix ruptured," Haycorn tells us. "Mr. Jiang will be in the hospital for a couple days, then he'll be home recovering for a week or two."

The worry washes off of everyone's face. Patrick keeps blinking like he's trying not to cry. Then I start blinking a lot too. Mr. Jiang is the nicest teacher I've ever had. In fact, he's more than a teacher. He's like a real human being.

"Which one of you called 9-1-1?" Principal Haycorn asks. We all point to Max, who's standing in the corner sobbing. "Smart thinking," he says as he passes her a tissue box. "You're a real hero."

Max wipes away her tears. "I'm just glad he's going to be okay." She takes a tissue and blows her nose so loud that it sounds like a Mack truck backfiring. Normally, that's the sort of thing that we'd all make fun of. Today, no one says anything.

At lunch Ramen reenacts the time his father had a heart attack and his mother took him to the hospital emergency room. However, it wasn't a heart attack at all — the diagnosis was heartburn.

"I'm not giving up my jalapeños!" Ramen starts yelling, imitating his dad.

I've seen this show before, so instead I watch Max sitting alone on the back stairs outside the auditorium. Except for her electric blue shoelaces, she's wearing all black. If she sees me, she doesn't let on.

I take a deep breath.

"Hey," I say as I approach. Max looks up from her taquitos. "Mr. Jiang was lucky you were there."

Max just nods.

There is a long silence between us.

"I'm sorry I thought you were a boy. Really."

"You hurt my feelings, Marley," Max says. "First by not even noticing I'm a girl, then by saying all that thoughtless stuff."

"I know, I know," I groan. "I said a lot of boneheaded things." She doesn't reply, but instead, just stares right at me. I don't know what I'm supposed to say. What more does she want? I've already said sorry. Max is so sensitive. When kids make fun of me or say mean things, I just ignore it. It doesn't bother me. Well, not that much.

"What do you want me to do?" I finally ask.

Max thinks this over. "I don't know. Not be a jerk, I guess."

I don't consider myself a jerk. Digger, Stanford, the Gorn — now those are jerks!

I shrug. "I'll try," I say. "Hey, you were great yesterday. None of us guys knew what to do."

Max lets out a long sigh. "I've seen something like that happen before, only it wasn't appendicitis, it was a heart attack. Everyone was so shocked that it took forever for someone to even call 9-1-1."

"Did the person live?" I ask.

Max looks incredibly sad. For the first time I notice how small she is. "No," she says softly. "My dad died."

Neither one of us moves. Finally, we hear Ramen shouting, "Hey, you nerf-herding bantha poodoo, stop playing statue and come join me. I'm lonely!"

Both of us let out some nervous laughter as he continues to hurl *Star Wars* insults our way. Then I help Max gather her lunch and we head back to the shade of the Tragic Tree, and the broken bench, and Ramen, who is waiting for us.

CAPTAIN'S LOG

Rift between crew members addressed.

14.

"How did you know what to do? You were amazing, like on that reality show, *Help, Someone Save Me!*"

Ramen won't stop quizzing Max as she tries to eat her sandwich. It looks like a car ran over it, but she claims that Cuban sandwiches are supposed to be flat.

"I would have just froze," Ramen tells her.

"You did," I point out.

"So did you," he shoots back.

I want to tell Ramen to shut up, but he won't. So instead, I try to change the subject. "Who do you think will be our AV teacher while Mr. Jiang is away?"

"Haven't you heard?" Ramen says between slurps of noodles. "We have to take Mrs. Wilder's class."

"What?!" I shout. "Noooo, not that!" I kick the Tragic Tree, then instantly feel bad, both for the tree and for my foot, which now hurts.

"Not what?" Max asks.

"Wilder teaches sixth-period Home Sciences," I explain. Max looks stricken. "I know! It's going to be torture. Hey, can you teach Ramen and me how to program the LED board?"

"Oh, the LED board," Max says. "I'm sorry for what I put on it. I was trying to be funny."

"What was funny?" Ramen asks. " 'Go, Tiggy'?"

"It was sort of rude," I tell her.

"What was rude?" Ramen asks. "The tiger? Max, did you make it do something rude?"

"It was pretty bad," Max admits.

"What? What?" Ramen asks. "Was there a boy on the LED board? Ohmygosh, did Tiggy eat the boy? He ate the boy, didn't he?"

"I had tried to tell you I was sorry," I tell Max. "You didn't need to say that thing on the board about me."

"What thing?" Ramen asks. "What did the board say?"

I turn to him. "Max programmed it to say 'Marley Sandelski is a loser.' "

"Is that all?" Ramen looks disappointed. "We already knew that."

"Are we even now?" Max asks.

I laugh. "Yeah, I guess so."

After school I stop by Sweeteria. I watch as the lady scoops my mint chocolate chip ice cream into the cone.

She looks like a grandma. Sometimes she gives me a double scoop, but only charges me for a single. I always make sure to thank her for it.

The bell on the door rings and I turn around in time to see the Gorn slither into the shop. I've never seen one of them alone, or even two of them without the third. They must do everything together, from getting the same haircuts — well, shaved heads — to wearing the same football jerseys and jeans. Heck, they even have the same dumb swagger. I guess brothers are like that. They all wave to me and blow kisses while I watch them slip some candy bars into their pockets. The bell on the door rings as they leave. Their stealing spree must have taken less than twenty seconds.

"Is there anything else I can get you?" the ice-cream lady asks as she hands me my cone. The bun on the very top of her head makes it look like she's balancing a scoop of vanilla ice cream.

I shake my head and pay, being sure to thank her. Before I go, I leave an extra two dollars by the cash register. It's all I have. It won't cover everything the gruesome Gorn got, but at least it's something.

I head home. It's Friday. You would think there would be no homework on Friday, but nooooo, I have math worksheets and that stupid family essay, both due on Monday. Why do teachers do that? Do they think we don't have a life? Things to do? Places to go? Suddenly, I remember that I don't have anything to do, or any places to go. I don't have a life. Then I think about Mr. Jiang. I hope he gets better soon.

Last year, I drew a picture of Mr. Jiang in my old Captain's Log. I made him a crew member of the *Enterprise*, not a guest star. He's that cool.

When I get home Dad's climbing down the ladder. He changed the marquee for the Saturday matinee. "Hey, Marley!" he calls out.

I rush up to him and give him a long hug. He hugs me back. "What's this all about?" he asks.

"Just happy to see you," I tell him.

CAPTAIN'S LOG

Recalibrated foe status of new crew member. Observed the Gorn in action. They are predators and thieves. Prognosis for Chief Engineer looks good.

15.

"Digger, please stay after class."

I stop and pretend to tie my shoe so I can listen in. "I just don't understand," Ms. McKenna's saying. Today she's wearing green Converse with plaid socks that match her scarf. "Digger, you do so well on your homework, but your quiz and test scores aren't very high. Do you have anxiety when you take a test?"

"I guess so," Digger mumbles. He runs his fingers through his hair and it stands up straight like he's been electrocuted. "Yeah, that's it."

"Well," Ms. McKenna smiles broadly, "I have just the thing for that! Here's a little warm fuzzy. This will help calm you down *and* send you good vibes."

Digger leaves, clutching something in the palm of his hand. I follow him. He stops at the dented metal trash can in the hallway before moving on. Resting on top of the garbage is a small yellow fluff ball with googly eyes and cardboard feet. It must be Digger's warm fuzzy. I scoop it up and slip it into my pocket.

"Looking for lunch?" asks a familiar voice. I turn around as students scatter. The Gorn are rumbling toward me like dump trucks. I take off running, weaving in and out of clumps of kids. They follow me. Some girls scream as we push past them. Most just step aside. They've seen this before. They know the dance. As I near my destination, I don't bother to slow down. Instead I burst through the door and skid to a stop.

Everyone looks up from behind sewing machines.

"Ah," the ancient-looking teacher says. "You must be Marley. You're late. I'm Mrs. Wilder — welcome to Home Sciences."

She motions toward an empty seat. I sit, still panting. The girl next to me whispers, "Hi, Marley, my name is Emily Ebers!"

I nod and look around for the rest of the AV Club. They're scattered around the room and none look happy. Mrs. Wilder honks a bicycle horn to get our attention. "Class, eventually, we will use the sewing machines. But since we have Mr. Jiang's Technical Sciences students as our guests for the next couple of weeks, I've decided to deviate a little from our lesson plans. Everyone, please pair up."

Automatically, I start to head toward Ramen, but the girl next to me taps me on the shoulder. "Marley, would you be my partner?"

I stop. A girl wants to be my partner? I look around the room to see if this is a setup. Maybe someone paid her to ask me, and if I say yes the whole class will break out laughing. One time in elementary school a boy offered me a cookie. When I bit into it everyone started howling because it was a dog biscuit. I didn't want them to know how upset I was, so I ate the whole thing and pretended I liked it. Later, I threw up.

But this girl looks sincere, and she isn't offering me any food. Instead, she's smiling and waiting for my answer. "Luq," I blurt out. Shoot! Why am I speaking Klingon? "Uh, I mean, yes, okay, I'll do it," I stammer.

Just then, both Ramen and Max appear. "Hi, I'm Emily," the girl says to them. "Marley's going to be my partner!"

Ramen looks at her, then at me, then back at her. His eyes widen as he breaks into a smile. "Way to go," he whispers loudly. I try to ignore him even though he keeps nudging me.

"Hi, I'm Max and this joker is Ramen," Max explains to Emily.

I look at the both of them standing side by side. No wonder I thought Max was a boy; she's not like Emily, who's all girl-like. Emily has long brownish blonde hair that curls at the ends, and she's wearing a dress. Plus, she's got a green necklace on and dangly earrings. Just by looking at her you can tell that Emily Ebers is a girl.

Max turns to Ramen and slaps him on the back. "I guess we're stuck with each other. Come on, Wookiee, let's sit down."

Neither Troy nor Patrick have partners. They look at each other and shrug. Mrs. Wilder toots her horn again. "It looks like everyone's paired up. Okay! Well, I have something very special planned. You've all seen the show *Project Fashion Designer*, right?" Emily is nodding. "Well, we're going to have our own version with a runway show and actual judges!" Mrs. Wilder is so fired up by her own announcement that she starts clapping. Are teachers everywhere this weird, or is it just my school?

Some of the girls in the class start to talk excitedly. The AV Club members look like they've been struck mute by phasers.

"This should be fun," Emily says, turning toward me. "I'm glad you agreed to be my partner, Marley. I'm new to Rancho Rosetta." She has a really big smile. Plus, her eyes sparkle. I quickly look away. She's so pretty that it hurts to look at her.

Emily doesn't seem to notice that I'm picking at a hole in my jeans. I'm glad I'm sitting down so she can't see that my pants are way too short. She keeps talking. "*Project Fashion Designer* is one of my favorite television shows. What's your favorite TV show?"

"JIyajbe," I say.

Stop. Speaking. Klingon. Gotta get a hold of myself.

"I mean, uh, um, *Star Trek*," I mumble. "I like *Star Trek: TOS*. That means The Original Series. QaStaH nuq?"

"Oh! Is that the show where the women wear those cute minidresses and have their hair in updos?"

"HISlaH! Um, that means, yes. You don't happen to speak Klingon, do you?" I ask meekly.

"Marley, Emily, face front, please." Mrs. Wilder peers over her horn-rimmed glasses. They look like my Benjamin Franklin ones. I wonder if she was his teacher too? She certainly seems old enough.

As Mrs. Wilder starts scribbling on the board in that uptight teacher handwriting they all have, a wad of paper hits me in the head. I turn around. Ramen gives me a thumbs-up. I try not to grin. We both know I've hit the jackpot with Emily.

Class is going by pretty fast. My heart keeps racing. I'm hyperaware that there's a cute girl sitting next to me who doesn't hate me. Emily smells good, like soap or sunshine or something. I try to be stealth as I sniff my armpit. Maybe I should use deodorant, especially since the Gorn have been chasing me even more lately.

The bell rings. Emily stands up. She's almost as tall as me. "Well, it was nice to meet you, Marley. I look forward to being your partner!"

Suddenly, I am aware that I'm wearing my Spock shirt with the spaghetti stain. I put my hand over the stain, but now it looks like I'm saying the pledge of allegiance. "Affirmative," I say.

As I watch Emily leave the room, Ramen and Max join me. "She's new to the school," I tell them.

Ramen makes kissy noises in my ear. I shove him away. Max shakes her head. "What's the big deal about her?" she asks.

"Girls who are new are always interesting," Ramen says as he watches Emily leave.

"I'm new here," Max reminds him.

"Then I take it back," he says.

Max bristles. "Can one of you please explain to me what guys think makes a girl attractive?"

Ramen and I are silent as we mull this over. He speaks first. "Well, she's gotta be hot."

"Define 'hot,' " Max demands.

"It's, you know, hot," Ramen says. "Nice looking. Nice hair, nice skin, and she has to smell nice —"

"Smile," I add. "She has to have a great smile."

". . . no visible scars or oozing wounds or anything," Ramen throws in. "And tall. I like my women tall. Like a supermodel tall."

"I don't care how tall the girl is," I say, "but she needs to have a good appearance, like she cares about how she looks. She can't be a slob."

"This coming from you?" Max says, laughing. "You're a slob. Your hair's so shaggy I can't even see your face, and you slouch when you walk." When Ramen starts snickering, she turns to him. "And you, you're a short *Star Wars* geek, but you like hot supermodels with no wounds?"

"Yeah, so what?" he says defensively. "What do you look for in a guy?"

Max hesitates, then tells us, "He's got to be confident, and smart, and funny. It doesn't hurt if he looks great. You know, good hair, clean, strong jaw, nice eyes, killer physique . . ." As she goes on and on, I feel myself shrinking. Great. It's official. No girl will ever be interested in me.

But wait! Emily Ebers was nice to me, and she's a girl — a really nice and pretty girl. Maybe there's hope for me yet.

CAPTAIN'S LOG

Temporarily docked on strange new planet. Friendly alien has offered to serve as a guide.

16.

Mom gets out her golf clubs as I deliver Dad's dinner. He insists on staying in the projection booth even though he's spliced together the twenty-minute reels, then stacked them onto two platters to feed into the projector. This way he doesn't have to change reels in the middle of the film. Technically, once my father's threaded the projector and the movie is running, he could leave, as long as he's back before the film ends. But Dad is old school.

I love watching him work. When the big boxes of film arrive, the first thing he does is inspect the reels. Sometimes, I do too. Every now and then he lets me thread the projector. Once the feature film is playing, Dad goes into the theater to check the focus and make sure the sound is okay. Then he heads back into his booth. If people want popcorn or a soda during the movie, they just get it themselves and leave the money in the film canister on the counter. Everything's a dollar to make it easier on the customers.

Cedra double-parks in front of the Rialto, and Mom and I climb in. "Hi, Patrice. Hey, Marley," Cedra says. "Want to see my new tattoo?" She holds out her arm. "It's a hummingbird," she tells Mom. "It's about the size of a half-dollar. Nick did it." Cedra's boyfriend is a tattoo artist.

"I'm sure it's lovely," Mom tells her.

Cedra smiles. "It is," she says, putting the van into gear and taking off.

She drops us off at the Arroyo Seco Golf Course. "I'll be back at eight thirty," Cedra says before peeling out of the parking lot.

I carry Mom's clubs for her as she gets her tokens for the golf ball machine. I like to listen to the balls drop into the metal bucket. Mom does too. She can tell when there are too many, too few, or just the right amount.

The driving range isn't very crowded. As always, we go to the second level. It looks over a great green expanse of grass and is lit so brightly that I always squint at first. Mom's favorite tee is open. She begins to stretch to warm up, then pulls her nine iron out of her bag. I set the bucket of balls behind her to the left. Using a golf club head, Mom finds the plastic tee sticking up from the ragged patch of Astroturf. She places the first ball down, sets her stance, and takes a practice swing. Satisfied, she reconfigures her position and brings the nine iron back over her shoulder.

Whack!

Mom's ball sails across the driving range. "Well?" she asks.

"Ninety yards," I tell her.

"What was my trajectory?"

"Low with a slight curve to the left."

She shakes her head. "I can do better."

I nod, even though she can't see me. She can do better.

In the next hour, Mom uses her nine and six irons, working her way to her fairway wood. Dad bought her the clubs for their fifteenth wedding anniversary last year. Mom cried when she got them and hugged him so hard that I thought she was hurting him, but apparently she wasn't.

"Two hundred yards," I call out. As she sets up her next ball, I doodle a picture of Emily Ebers in my Captain's Log. As an afterthought, I add Vulcan ears. She makes an attractive Vulcan.

"Marley, hand me my driver," Mom says. I fetch it from her bag.

Next to us, a plump, dark-haired woman wearing shorts and an electric green shirt is watching Mom swing. I sit on the bench and drink a Pepsi. Even though I'm not allowed to drink soda at home, Mom lets me have one here. I have a stash of quarters just for the soda machine.

"Your mom's really good," the woman says. I nod.

My mother comes over and sits next to me.

"I was just telling your son that you're really good," the lady says.

"Why, thank you," Mom replies as she takes a sip from her water bottle. "I've been at this for years."

"Me too. But I'm still so bad at golf, I may as well be playing blind."

Mom laughs. "Well, that's how I play."

"Excuse me?"

"I am blind," my mother says.

The woman instantly reddens. "Ohmygosh, I am so sorry!"

A patient smile crosses my mother's face. I've seen it many times before. "Why are you sorry? It's not your fault."

"Is it hard to golf?" The lady starts speaking loudly. "Can you actually golf, like on the course?"

"I may be blind, but I'm not uncoordinated," my mother quips. "And yes, I'm actually part of a foursome and we golf once a week."

The lady rises and puts out her hand to shake Mom's, then abruptly pulls it back. "It was an honor to meet you. You are a true inspiration."

For a moment, I'm glad my mother can't see, because the look of pity the lady is giving her is outrageous. Lots of people look at Mom like that. Or they just stare. Others run up to her and do things like try to walk her across the street, when truly my mother is probably more capable than 99% of the population.

As the woman scurries away, Mom begins gathering her clubs. "Okay, Marley, are you ready to head home with an inspiration?"

We wait a beat, then both break out laughing.

School's been dragging on for almost a month and I've fallen into my morning routine.

1. Force myself out of bed.
2. Eat breakfast.
3. Walk one block.
4. Wait for Digger.
5. Wait for Digger.
6. Hand Digger his own copy of my history homework.
7. Wait for Digger to leave.
8. Head to school.

Digger's slime. Still, I can't bring myself to tell anyone about him. My stomach is in a knot every Tuesday and Thursday morning when I hand over the history homework. I always avoid looking directly at Digger. His ice blue eyes could freeze your soul.

I couldn't sleep all night. Over and over I practiced what I was going to say to Digger, and now that he's standing in front of me, I wish I were back in bed, under the covers.

"What?" he asks. He's in his normal bad mood. His hair is going in twelve different directions at once and looks like a forest fire. "Where is it?"

I tighten my grip on my backpack.

"Why?" I ask. "Why should I do your homework? I don't think I want to do it anymore."

Digger smiles and shakes his head. "Marley, Marley, Marley," he says, like he's talking to a toddler. "This is not about what you want, but about what you will do. And you will do what I say because if you don't, there will be grave consequences."

My throat is dry. "Like what?" I squawk.

"You really don't want to know," he says.

Digger's right. I don't really want to know. He's capable of anything, like the time in elementary school when he got that really smart girl expelled.

I hand him my homework.

When I get to my locker Max and Ramen are blocking it. "What?" I ask. Neither says anything. "Ramen, I've got to get to my stuff. Move," I order.

Ramen looks at Max. She shrugs. He steps aside. Water is pouring out of my locker like it's Niagara Falls. Quickly, I try my combination. Shoot! The lock's been jammed with gum. When I finally get it open, everything inside is wet and ruined. A small plastic tube is stuck in one of the locker vents. Whoever did this must have pumped the water in through that.

"I've got a spare notebook if you need one," Max offers. Good thing I keep my new Captain's Log on me. When I look up, the Gorn are there, snickering. Before they leave each punches me in the arm.

"Leave him alone!" Max yells, clenching her fists and marching toward them.

Ramen stops her. "Don't do it," he warns. He has to grab her arm and hold her back. "It'll only draw attention to you and then you'll be next on their list."

"You don't know that," Max says. Her eyes are ablaze.

"Yes I do!" Ramen spits back. "Because I was the one they used to punch before Marley tried to stop them."

CAPTAIN'S LOG

The enemy Gorn have infiltrated a satellite substation. Damage was minimal. However, the stigma of the attack remains.

It's lunchtime. Max is biting into lox and cream cheese on a bagel. "What are those little green balls?" Ramen is asking. "They look like those pill bugs. Are those pill bugs? Marley ate a worm once."

"It was an accident," I explain.

"These are capers," Max says, then takes another bite. "Hey, Marley, I think you should tell Principal Haycorn about those bullies."

I shake my head. "I've told you, it would just make things worse."

Ramen nods. "He's right for once. It's best for our kind to just grin and bear it. Or in this case, grimace and bear it."

Max huffs. "Batman would never do that. He'd fight the bad guys."

"Yeah, well, if I could, I'd transport all the bad guys out of here and into Klingon territory," I say sarcastically.

"Only, guess what, Max? My phaser and transporter are in the shop."

Ramen snorts. "I'd lend you a lightsaber, but all of mine are recharging."

We both break out laughing, but Max just scowls. "I don't like it that they hit you, Marley."

I sober up. "You think I do? You think it's fun for me?"

Max chews slowly. "I just think you ought to tell someone. Maybe Mr. Jiang when he gets back," she says. "Or a teacher. Principal Haycorn. Someone."

"I'll think about it," I tell her, even though I know I won't. If I did that, the Gorn would track me down, rip me apart, stomp on my guts, and *then* make my life miserable.

"Hey, you know that Emily girl you're partners with in Home Sciences?" Ramen asks.

"What about her?" I ask, trying to make my voice sound normal.

Ramen lets out a whistle. He's really good at making noises. You should hear his imitation of an old-fashioned locomotive gaining speed, then crashing into a mountain.

"Emily has P.E. the same time I do," Max volunteers. "She's about as coordinated as I am, which means that neither of us should be looking for careers as athletes."

"I can't believe you have her for your partner," Ramen tells me. "You have all the luck."

"Gee, thanks," Max says snidely. She tosses a caper at him.

"Aw, I didn't mean it like that," Ramen backtracks. "You're an okay partner, even if you're all Batman. I'll bet Emily is into *Star Wars*."

"Right." Max joins Ramen under the Tragic Tree. "Dream on. I'll bet that Emily doesn't even know who Princess Leia is. She probably thinks she's a Disney princess."

"I'm sure she knows who Princess Leia is. Everyone does," Ramen argues.

While Ramen and Max engage in a staredown, I ignore them. They're ridiculous. Besides, I have something more interesting to think about . . . Emily Ebers.

CAPTAIN'S LOG

Ignored bad advice from crew member regarding enemy. Contemplating significance of friendly new alien.

In history class Ms. McKenna collects our homework. I always get 100%, but there is little joy in that, knowing that Digger is getting 100% too.

Ms. McKenna is telling the class about a place called Colonial Williamsburg, where people dress up the way they did in the eighteenth century. She's wearing an old bonnet as she shows us some photos of someone milking a cow. I'd like to visit there someday. I could wear my Benjamin Franklin jacket and glasses.

Suddenly, Ms. McKenna starts doing a rap about Williamsburg. It's so bad it hurts.

> *Don't be a fool,*
> *History can be cool.*
> *Let learning be a tool.*
> *Sha boom, sha boom!*
> *In Williamsburg you can see*

A Colonial city
And how it used to be.
Sha boom, sha boom!

After school, I climb the stairs to the apartment and flop on the couch. Mom puts her Italy book on pause so we can talk. "How's school?" she asks, giving me a hug.

"Fine."

"Have you made any new friends?"

"Well, I guess so. There's this new kid, Max, that Ramen and I eat lunch with."

"What's he like?" she asks as she straightens the pillows on the couch.

"Max is a girl."

Instantly, Mom lights up. "A girl? Well, tell me all about this Max!"

"It's not like that," I moan. I'm sorry that I even brought it up. "She's in AV Club and not really like a girl-girl. Max is more like one of the guys."

"Well, you should invite Max to the theater sometime," Mom says, adding, "I promise not to embarrass you."

"Who's not going to embarrass whom?" Dad asks as he comes into the room. He's carrying a box of paperwork.

My father has an office downstairs off the concession stand, but he likes to do the accounting in the apartment. It's interesting to watch him hunched over the kitchen table with a calculator. It's like there are two different Dads: the movie buff and the businessman. After he counts the money, he slips a thick rubber band around the bills, then puts the bundle into a Ziploc bag and places it in our freezer until he has a chance to go to the bank.

"Marley has a friend who's a girl," Mom tells him.

"Marley," Dad says, hardly hiding his grin, "who's this girl that has your mother all in a dither?"

I shake my head. "Just a new kid. It's nothing. Can I go now?"

"Be back in time for dinner," Mom tells me.

I wander around downtown Rancho Rosetta for a while. I wave to Libby at Stout's Coffee Shop, and stop in at RadioShack. Mr. Min shows me the new cell phones. They do everything. It would be so cool to have one, and it wouldn't matter that I don't have anyone to call — I could just play the games and stuff.

As I head toward the Dinosaur Farm toy store to see if the new juggling balls have come in, I suddenly spy Emily Ebers! She's feeding coins into a parking meter. Wait. That's odd. Now she's putting money into all the meters up and down Mission Street. When she looks in my direction, I take off running and don't stop until I get to Sweeteria. Mom doesn't have to know.

As I leave with my ice-cream cone, I spot Stanford with his pals heading toward me. Do basketball players always travel in packs? I turn in the other direction and see the Gorn coming my way. Luckily, they only harass me at school. Still, I duck into a store and crouch down.

"Do you have an appointment?" the lady asks. She's tall and has short hair that looks metallic, like bronze, and she has the same bemused look that Uhura, the communications officer of the USS *Enterprise*, often wears. They could be sisters.

I stand up and look around. There's a sign above the counter that says SALON FERRANTE. "Um, no," I say as I begin to back out of the place. "I was just —"

She smiles at me. "No problem. Drop by anytime. Ask for Mimi. I specialize in making good-looking guys look even better."

I try not to blush when she winks at me. When I leave, I notice my hand is all cold and sticky. I'm still holding my ice-cream cone. It's practically melted. I look for a trash can. Just then, I hear someone say, "There he is, get him!"

There's no time to look. Instinctively, I start to run. I can hear the Gorn grunting as they chase me. I toss the cone into the street and dodge an old lady who yells, "Young man, you're a litterbug!" Then she yells at the Gorn, "You big boys — this is a shopping area, not a racetrack!"

I run past Stahl Miller stationery store and City Hall. Mr. Min and I wave to each other as I run past RadioShack. I don't stop until I'm at the Rialto.

"Whoa, slow down, Marley," Mom says as I burst into the apartment. "Your timing is impeccable. Dinner's ready. Here, take this plate up to your father."

I nod and run the broccoli noodle casserole up to the projection booth. Then I trek down to the basement and slip on my Spock ears to decompress. I've decided to call this the Transporter Room, because this is where I need to be when I want to escape.

CAPTAIN'S LOG

Red alert. The Gorn have expanded their base of attack.

20.

After P.E. I'm heading to the locker room when I hear Coach Martin say, "Sandelski! Get back here."

Great. What have I done now? Or what haven't I done? Wait, I can think of a few things.

1) I ran with the basketball instead of dribbling.
2) I tried to make a shot, but it got blocked by the shortest kid in the class.
3) I fouled my own teammate.

"Yeah," I say, giving Coach a preemptive glare.

"I saw you running yesterday," he says.

"Running?"

"Around town." Coach Martin's beloved whistle hangs around his neck. He's wearing a new Dodgers cap. He must have hundreds of them. "You should go out for track. How long have you been running?"

"I'm not a runner," I tell him. Though that's not true. I started running away from the bullies when I was in elementary school. I'm still running from them.

"Well, you *should* be a runner," Coach Martin says. "You're fast, Sandelski. Listen up, okay?"

Why do adults say "listen up"? What exactly is that supposed to mean?

"Sandelski! Are you with me?"

I nod.

"You're doing pretty poorly in P.E." I nod again. I know. Everyone knows. "As a matter of fact, you're barely pulling a C grade. However, we have the Tiggy Tiger Turkey Trot coming up. That's where the middle school students compete in a 2K." Why is he telling me this? "You compete and I'll give you an A for the semester. You don't even have to win or place. Just compete, okay?"

I shrug.

"Think about it. Will you at least think about it, Sandelski?"

"Okay," I say. "I'll think about it."

I get to the locker room just in time for the Gorn to push me into the shower with my gym clothes on. Even though this is getting old, a few of the boys laugh, but most turn away. They've seen it before.

21.

"Hi, Marley!"

Emily Ebers is saying hi to me?

"NuqneH," I answer. Oh no! I'm speaking Klingon again.

"Excuse me?" Emily says as I take my seat next to her.

"Greetings, earthling!" I shout. Shoot. Why am I shouting?

"I'm so excited about today," Emily gushes. "Marley, are you excited? Today Mrs. Wilder gives us our *Project Fashion Designer* assignments!"

"Affirmative," I answer. It's wonderful and awful to talk to Emily. I can't even look at her without feeling queasy, like my guts are going to pop out. I've been trying to figure out what color her eyes are. I think they're brown with some green, like that necklace she always wears. But whenever Emily looks directly at me, I turn away for fear that I'll say something stupid, or fall down, or drool.

"Class, your attention!" Mrs. Wilder toots her horn. Emily whips around to face the teacher. "Each of you is teamed up with one other student. Your assignment is to make an outfit that looks like couture. That is, a custom-made design." Emily lets out a little squeak. "And here's what you will be using for your creations."

Everyone breaks out laughing when Mrs. Wilder holds up black plastic trash bags. Emily leans in toward me and whispers, "This is going to be so fun!" Her arm touches mine and now it's my turn to squeak.

Mrs. Wilder continues, "Together you will design and create your outfits. One person from each team will tell the judges about the creation, while the other models it."

We collect our garbage bags and get to work. Emily is sketching what looks like a dress. I just sit and watch. She seems to know what she's doing, but even if she didn't, I'd still stare at her. She bites her lower lip when she's concentrating. When she looks up at me, I quickly turn away and pretend to be interested in a scab on my arm.

"I love clothes," Emily explains. "I get a lot of fashion magazines like *Gamma Girl*, so I kinda know what's in and what's out."

"Buy' ngop . . . er, that's great!"

I'm wearing my good Spock shirt today, the one without the spaghetti stain. Only now I notice it's slightly pink because Mom doesn't separate the laundry by color, for obvious reasons. I'm also wearing my only pair of jeans that aren't too short. I get most of my clothes at Out of the Closet, a secondhand shop on Fair Oaks. For the first time, I wish I had enough money to shop at the Paradise Mall in Pasadena where all the rich kids go.

"Uh, what are we going to make?" I ask. When the sentence comes out in English and not Klingon, I am relieved.

"A gown," Emily says brightly as she stares off in the distance. She has long eyelashes. "A beautiful flowing gown." I follow her gaze, but all I see is a poster of a sewing machine with the headline SEW RIGHT. WATCH YOUR FINGERS. Emily continues, "It's going to be amazing, with an empire waist and a long train."

"You'd look good in that," I say, even though I have no idea what she's talking about.

Suddenly, Emily snaps out of her daydream and turns serious. Instantly, my heart stops. What? What have I said?

"Well, the thing is," she says slowly, "that the dress should be draped on a model, like on that show *Hot Couture Creations*. You have seen *Hot Couture Creations*, haven't you?" I start to shake my head no, then nod, making it look like I'm drawing a circle with my head. "I can't very well create it on myself. You wouldn't mind, would you?"

"Mind what?" I ask.

"Being the model," she says. "I can create the dress on you!"

My body seizes up. "No, no, no," I quickly correct her. "You be the model. It's a dress. You're a girl."

"Oh, please, Marley, please," she begs. Emily's eyes grow big. "I've always wanted to create a custom gown on a real live model, like the professionals. And since I know how it should look, I have to be the one to design it and then drape it on you. Also, that way I can be the person to talk about the creation of the gown while you model." She pauses. "Unless you have experience with making clothes?"

"I can fix a projector and can program the cafeteria LED board," I begin to babble. "I know how to run the PA system and can get any DVD player to work. Did you know that the original name for the USS *Enterprise* was *Yorktown* —"

"Marley, please stand up," Emily says as she reaches for the tape measure.

I do as I'm told.

In a normal universe, Emily Ebers putting her arms around me to take my measurements would be the highlight of my life. Only, I don't think I'm in a normal universe anymore.

"You don't mind, do you?" she asks. Her eyes are sparkling and drawing me in. I try to activate my force field, but it's disabled.

"I don't mind," I hear myself saying.

The bell rings all too soon, and everyone heads out. That's when I notice Emily has left something behind. *Gamma Girl* magazine. I pick it up and run out to give it to her, but she's already disappeared into the crowd.

CAPTAIN'S LOG

Friendly alien left behind an interplanetary manual. Will need to translate it for future reference.

I got a B-plus on my family essay. My English teacher, Ms. Klein, is telling me, "Marley, you would have gotten a higher grade had you written three pages, as you were assigned."

"But there aren't three pages worth of stuff to say about my family," I try to explain. "We're pretty boring."

"You could have talked more about the Rialto," Ms. Klein says. She's wearing a headband over her blondish hair and looks like she's in high school. "I love the Rialto! Everyone does."

Yeah, right. If everyone who says they love the Rialto showed up, then maybe Mom and Dad wouldn't be so worried about going out of business.

"Marley, to live in a historic landmark is amazing." Ms. Klein tucks a pencil behind her ear. She doesn't notice that she already has one there. "I really wish you had written more about it."

"Could I . . . could I still write about it?" I ask. "For extra credit maybe?"

It's worth asking. I'm not a straight-A student, but I'm close. I don't think that they should count your P.E. grade as part of your GPA.

Ms. Klein shakes her head, and I think she's going to say no until I hear, "Give me more than one page, and make it good, Marley. I want more than just words, I want insight. Then, after I read your paper, I'll consider giving you extra credit."

Even though the Transporter Room is cavernous, it's cozy. My *Star Trek* action figures are mingling with the warm fuzzies that I've rescued from the trash can outside Ms. McKenna's classroom. They seem to be getting along.

I can hear one of Mom's students assaulting the piano. Most of her students are little kids, although her newest student is an adult — Mr. Alan from the post office. When he finally stops, the silence is bliss. I open my Captain Kirk notebook and begin my rough draft. Later, I'll use Mom's computer and type it up.

MY FAMILY
by Marley Sandelski

Is it weird to live in a theater? A place where for almost 100 years shows and movies have been held? Not for me, Marley Sandelski. The Rialto Theater is my home. I've lived here all my life. My family owns the theater. My father runs the theater, and my mother plays the organ.

There are others who live here too. But they live on the silver screen. Great actors and actresses from classic movies. They visit us all the time. Some stay longer than others. Some make return visits. Some people say there's a ghost who lives here, but I've never seen or heard him. Even if there was a ghost, I wouldn't be afraid. Ghosts are just people who are having trouble transitioning from one life to another, as if their transporter malfunctioned.

My family clips coupons, buys used clothes, and rarely goes out to nice dinners. Never once have we been on a vacation, unless you count the time when I was nine and we went to the Wilmer Eye Clinic in Baltimore. We stayed in a hotel and even ate at Red Lobster. My parents were happy and hopeful. Later, the mood changed. I'm not sure what the doctors told my mother, but it was the only time I've seen her cry. Dad cried too. So did I, but only because I was scared to see my parents so upset.

Every night after the Rialto is closed, my father plays a film just for my mother. The two of them sit in the front row of the empty theater and snuggle as he narrates the scenes. If she's close enough to the screen, Mom can see bits of light and fuzzy images.

Tonight, Dad's screening <u>Casablanca</u> again. He can see a film a hundred times and never get tired of it. Mom's seen the movie before too, but I don't think that matters to them. It's like they've created their own little nest here.

Sometimes I join my parents and listen to my father. I close my eyes and try to imagine what my mother sees. When my dad's narrating, it's almost better than the movie itself. If only our lives were half as good as what plays at the Rialto.

23.

The Gorn wait for me every day at 3 P.M., although I get the weekends off. Apparently, it's no longer enough that their punches land on me during school, or that they've shoved me into my locker so many times you can see a dent in the shape of my body. Now chasing me around town has become their extracurricular activity. I don't mind, though. In a weird way, I sort of like it. Not the chasing part, but the running part. When I run my mind clears and my body feels light, like I'm flying. It's the best feeling ever, as if I've gone into warp drive and the laws of physics don't apply to me.

"See you tomorrow, Marley," Emily is saying as she puts her things into her purple backpack. I've noticed that she changes backpacks to match her clothes. "We'll start draping the dress on you tomorrow."

"Maj!" I tell her. "I mean, good! Maj is Klingon, and you're not an intergalactic alien and —" Rats. She's gone.

I could kick myself. I sound so stupid. In all the old movies, the guys are always so smooth and witty.

I look over at Ramen, who is batting his eyelashes and kissing the back of his hand. When I try to wave him off, Max laughs even harder. I join the two of them and we head out. As I pass Emily at her locker I make a mental note of the number. Hey! She has an orange locker and so do I. That must mean something, right?

We keep walking until Max stops and says, "Uh-oh."

Ramen bumps into her, then echoes, "Uh-oh."

I don't have to look to know what they are uh-oh-ing about. Instead, I hoist my backpack over my shoulder and say, "*Adios, amigos.*"

"Get him," the Gorn leader yells.

And so begins my afternoon run. As always, I ditch my backpack behind the air-conditioning unit. I'll get it later. It's sort of liberating, racing around town. If my tormentors had half a brain between them, they'd know that I run the same way every day — even on the days no one is chasing me. No matter how I bad I feel, I feel better after a run. I need to run the way Captain Kirk needs the *Enterprise*. It's just part of who I am.

As I cover my route, I wave to Mimi at the hair place. I wave to Mr. Min at RadioShack, and to Officer Ramsey at Stout's Coffee Shop, and Dave at the Dinosaur Farm. On occasion I'll see Stanford or someone else from school — on those days I change course to avoid them. I usually elude the Gorn at the park where they're easily distracted by the swing set, an errant tennis ball, or a squirrel. Then, even though no one is chasing me, I keep on running just for the fun of it.

I swing back around to school to get my backpack, then slow when I near the Rialto. Dad is putting up a *Mary Poppins* poster in the glass case. "I'm going to try a Family Matinee on Saturdays," he says as he closes the case and locks it. "Think that'll bring people in?"

"It's worth a try," I tell him. My father is always coming up with new ideas to increase business.

I grab an apple and head downstairs. Mom's telling a student, "Penny, there's no need to attack the piano keys. You'll just wear out your fingers if you keep doing that. Try a lighter touch."

When I get to the end of the hallway I push the door open and step into the Transporter Room. Someday I'll rig the door so that when it opens, the theme from *Star Trek* plays. I settle into my captain's chair, munching on my apple and studying Emily's *Gamma Girl*. There's an article about "The Perfect Boyfriend." A photo takes up one whole page. The caption reads, "Seth is wearing distressed jeans and a rust-colored polo shirt, topped off with a B-Man jacket from RX59 — where all the cool kids shop."

I set the magazine aside and I put on my Benjamin Franklin jacket and glasses. Oh wait, can't forget the

Spock ears. Math is up first, then science homework. English is just a review of vocabulary words. I always do well on those. Now history. I save history for last since it's my favorite subject.

I turn to page 124. After I write the answers to the questions, I make a second copy for Digger, making sure to change my handwriting. I toy with the idea of writing down the wrong answers. The very thought of it warms me until I head back to reality. To do something like that would be worse than death. Whereas the rotten Gorn are likely to beat me into a pulp, Digger is far more dangerous. Once I saw a boy get so flustered when Digger looked at him that he bowed. Principal Haycorn practically does that too. Digger's family gives a lot of money to the school and even sponsors the Tiggy Tiger Turkey Trot. The new basketball hoops in the gym are courtesy of the Ronster family, and so is the fountain in the school courtyard and about half of the buildings.

"You live in the Rialto?" Digger said as I handed him the homework the other day. "It's fading fast and my father says it's an eyesore. He says that he may buy it out and put up a huge multiplex. That's where the money is. After all, who wants a crumbling theater no one goes to . . ."

For the first time I noticed that on the outside, the Rialto does look like it's crumbling. The paint is peeling, there's a wooden board over one of the upstairs windows, plus there are chips in the plaster like the place has leprosy. Is this how the rest of the world sees the Rialto? If only they would take the time to really look at it. I think they'd be surprised at how beautiful it is inside.

I remember what Digger said last: "... of course, my father always listens to me — we're really close. So I've told him to let the Rialto stand. For now."

I copy the last answer on my history homework onto Digger's paper. Then I turn off the light and head upstairs.

CAPTAIN'S LOG

Pressure from enemy forces continues to mount. Psychological attacks, as well as physical ones, appear to be on the upswing.

24.

A dress. Who would have ever thought that I'd be standing in the middle of a classroom wearing a dress?

"Stop fidgeting," Emily says. Even when she frowns, she's pretty. "Marley, if you don't stand still, I won't be able to do this."

I glance around the room. Max and Ramen are arguing in the corner. Ramen is looking as uncomfortable as me as Max winds miles of black electrical tape around him. On the other side of the room, Troy and Patrick are both wearing garbage bags. Only their heads stick out and they're trying to knock each other down.

Emily comes close and cuts two holes in a bag. Today, her hair smells like coconut. I wonder what my hair smells like. I hope it doesn't stink. Sometimes I forget to use shampoo. I make a mental note to wash my hair twice tonight.

"Okay, Marley, put your arms through the holes, but be careful, so you don't tear the plastic. Oh, and would you mind standing up straight?"

She steps back and looks me over. I try not to squirm as she circles around me. "I think a cinched waist would be best, don't you?"

I give her a halfhearted smile to indicate that perhaps we ought to give up, or at least maybe make a nice suit or something else. Or maybe we should switch and I should be the main designer and she should be the model. She could just tell me what to do.

Emily is not picking up on my signal. Instead, she continues circling. "Yes, a cinched waist and maybe a bow or a flower?"

I surrender and nod. I wouldn't do this for anyone but her. She is so nice. I know she would never write mean things on my locker or try to trip me. Emily actually says hi to me when she sees me around school. The first time she said, "Hi, Marley!" I was so stunned I shut my locker on my hand.

"Designers!" Mrs. Wilder toots her bicycle horn. I'll bet she's the sort of driver who honks all the time, even when no one else is around.

Patrick turns to Troy and says, "Did you fart? 'Cause if you farted inside that bag, it would be suicide."

Mrs. Wilder ignores him. It's weird. When someone

makes a really loud obnoxious joke, teachers pretend not to hear them. But when someone whispers something, they make sure you know they heard.

"You have four days left before the fashion show," Mrs. Wilder is saying. "I hope you are making the best use of your time, boys and girls."

Boys and girls? What grade does she think we are in?

Emily raises her hand. "Mrs. Wilder, what about accessories? Can we bring some from home?"

"Just the bags and tape," she answers.

"That's too bad," Emily tells me. "This gown would look good with a strand of pearls or a small hat with a feather."

"I have a feather hat," I blurt out. "I mean, I have a bunch of gowns and things, and there are even some hats with feathers." Emily gives me a quizzical look. "Well, they're not really mine," I struggle to explain. "They're old costumes from vaudeville shows and stuff. They're antiques."

Emily's eyes light up. "Oh! I'd love to see them sometime."

"You would?"

"Sure! I love vintage."

I feel light-headed and start to sit down, but Emily grabs my arm. "Don't sit, Marley. You might tear the gown."

She's staring at me and smiling. She has nice teeth. One's a little crooked, but it looks good. Everyone should have a crooked tooth like Emily's. I should floss more.

"Maj! I mean, um, well, okay, I guess," I say, hoping my voice doesn't crack. "How about tomorrow after school? I live in the Rialto Theater."

"You live in the Rialto? Ohmygosh, Marley, you are so cool!"

Emily Ebers thinks I'm cool and wants to come over?

I must be dreaming.

CAPTAIN'S LOG

The planets are realigning. Friendly alien has requested permission to explore Transporter Room. Permission granted.

I've never noticed how dusty the Transporter Room is. Everywhere I look is dirt and dust. Dust and dirt. It will take me forever to clean it, but it has to look good for Emily. It has to.

I pull out the hatboxes that were piled in the corner, then open the old steamer trunks and air out some of the gowns. One has sparkly beads all over it. It reminds me of Emily. All I have to do is think about her, and it feels like electricity is shooting through me, like the first time I saw Ricardo Montalban in *Star Trek II: The Wrath of Khan*. Only, Emily is way prettier and nicer than Khan, plus I doubt she's ever placed mind-controlling eels in any-one's ears.

I guess I'd better let my parents know she's coming over or else they'll be sure to embarrass me. The few times my father's met people from school, I could tell he was uncomfortable. Actually, he's uncomfortable with most people, unless he's talking films, like with some of the Rialto regulars. Then he can go on forever and it looks like he's actually having fun.

My mother's pretty outgoing. She has her golf buddies, and she talks to strangers all the time. Now and then she even talks to strangers when they don't want to talk to her. She doesn't see their discomfort or their looks of pity, but I do. Sometimes I wish that my family was normal, and that my mother wasn't blind, and that my father could go out without having a panic attack, and that I wasn't invisible. But maybe that's all about to change. Emily Ebers has noticed me.

I'm with my parents in the projection booth. My father has just dimmed the lights. Now he presses the button that makes the curtains part. As a preview for an early Hitchcock film, *Blackmail*, screens, I clear my throat. "Well, tomorrow a kid from one of my classes is going to come over."

"That's great, Marley. What's his name?" Mom asks.

"Emily."

"His name is Emily?" Dad says.

A smile alights on my mother's face. "A girl is coming over? Oh, Marley!"

I feel myself turning red. "It's nothing like that," I insist. "We're partners on a Home Sciences project, that's all."

"Well," Mom says, "we won't make a big deal about it, then."

I wake up early the next morning. Even though Home Sciences is last period, I don't want to be late for school. During P.E. we're playing basketball. I break a new school record for free throws . . . ten air balls.

The day drags. I get punched once, spit on twice, and shoved into my locker three times. Still, nothing can bring me down. Today Emily Ebers comes to visit!

Suddenly, it's sixth period.

"Looking good," Mrs. Wilder says as Emily puts some finishing touches on the gown. "You two should do well at the fashion show."

Emily beams. "You're a good sport to wear this, Marley. Not many boys would."

"That's a masterpiece of understatement," I answer, trying to sound like Cary Grant, the old-time movie star in *Bringing Up Baby*. He's one of Mom's favorite actors. My mother likes it when the actors have distinct accents, because she can visualize them better.

Emily is either too busy fiddling with the collar of the gown to notice my Cary Grant imitation, or too polite to mention it. I really can't tell what our dress looks like since I'm wearing it.

I have no clue what Max and Ramen's design looks like. They got permission to go outside and both are being supersecretive. As I survey the room, some of the other teams look panicked. One girl is almost crying as her partner laughs at their mess. It looks like it's gone through the garbage disposal. Patrick and Troy's garbage bags look exactly the same as the day they started — just two bags with two holes in it for their heads.

"Marley, am I still invited over after school today?" Emily asks as she stands back and looks me over.

"Affirmative!" I say too loudly.

"Should we walk together after school?"

The world stands still. Emily Ebers wants to walk home with me!!!

Wait.

The Gorn.

I can't ask Emily to run through town, but if we walk the Gorn might beat me up in front of her.

"I have something I have to do right after school," I say. This is true. I have to try to stay alive. "How about we meet in front of the Rialto at four o'clock?"

"That sounds perfect," Emily says brightly. "I'll see you then!"

26.

The Gorn are so predictable. As they lumber down the hallway, all three grin and crack their knuckles. It sounds like the rhythm section of a band without any rhythm. I wave hello before I take off running.

My tormentors seem sluggish today. They must have had the school pizza for lunch. I speed up anyway. I want to get home in time to get ready for Emily. Coach Martin is standing outside the gym holding his stopwatch as I run past.

I'm not even out of breath when I get to the Rialto. Both Mom and Dad are puttering around the apartment. On the kitchen table is a bowl of Doritos and a plate of Mom's oatmeal raisin cookies. When I open the refrigerator there's Pepsi.

"Thanks, Dad," I tell him.

"Don't thank me, thank your mother," he says, cocking his head toward her. "It was her idea."

I give Mom a huge hug.

I change into my clean VULCAN = VICTORY shirt, but then change back into what I wore to school. I wouldn't want Emily to think I changed because of her. Then I comb my hair and then muss it up. Same reason. I check the clock. It's 3:45 P.M. I am about to head down to the lobby, but first I need to write something.

CAPTAIN'S LOG

Expecting a visitor from another planet. Entering uncharted space. Anticipation high.

27.

"Hi, Marley!" Emily calls out. Her voice is almost more beautiful than the sound of the *Enterprise* going into warp speed, although, technically, something going into warp speed would not make any noise since there is no sound in space.

"YI'el!" I yell in Klingon. "Come in." I just stare at Emily until I notice a short Asian girl next to her, looking at me like I'm a Klingon.

"Marley, this is my best friend, Millicent Min," Emily says.

"Are you Mr. Min's daughter?" I ask.

"Very astute of you," she replies. I can't tell if she's being sarcastic.

"Millie loves old movies, so I invited her to join us. I hope that's okay with you."

Emily could have said, "I want the Vians to torture you

like they did to Spock. Is that okay with you?" and I would say yes.

"HISlaH, I mean, yes, I understand and it's fine! Affirmative!" Man, why do I have to sound like a dweeb? "Er, follow me. Beep. Beep. Beep."

I am acutely aware that I have way too much bounce in my step, so I try to adjust, but instead succeed only in shuffling my feet. Then I notice that my arms are swinging. Are they swinging too much? Shoot, I should have practiced walking!

I shove my hands into my pockets and lead them down the narrow stairwell to the Transporter Room. When I turn on the light, Emily gasps with delight. "Millie, look at all this . . . a throne!" It's a captain's chair, but I don't correct her.

"It is pretty cool down here," Millicent notes. I see her looking at my Benjamin Franklin jacket. "A place for everything, and everything in its place," she says as she picks up the Franklin biography I've checked out from the library. It's three days overdue because I want to reread parts of it.

"For every minute spent organizing, an hour is earned," I say, quoting him back to her.

Our eyes meet for a split second, then Emily calls out, "Millie, come over here. Look at this gown! And these hats!"

A feeling of pride washes over me as Emily and Millicent run around the Transporter Room yelling to each other at each discovery. Millicent seems especially interested in the old playbills and photos. Emily likes the dresses and costumes best.

"Can I try this on, Marley?" she asks, holding up the sparkly gown I thought she'd like.

"Sure," I tell her. "You can go into my mom's piano studio. She doesn't have any students right now."

Emily leaves Millicent and me alone. Even though she's small and skinny, Millicent Min makes me more nervous than the Gorn. I've heard that she's some sort of superstar genius or something. I try not to make any sudden moves.

"Are you that girl who's in high school?" I ask.

"There are lots of girls in high school," she says. Her enunciation is even better than Ms. Vracin's, my elementary school speech teacher. "But if you mean, 'Are you the freakishly smart girl who's supposed to be in seventh grade but is a senior in high school?' Then yes. That would be me. You are correct."

"I didn't mean to be rude," I say defensively. I wonder if she's going to tell Emily that I'm rude.

Millicent's shoulders droop slightly, then she straightens up. "I'm sorry, but it's just that so many people make fun of me. I thought that's what you were doing."

"I wouldn't do that. Honest."

She offers me a small smile. "No," she says, "I don't think you would. I really like all this stuff you have here. The Rialto is so remarkable. I've come here with my grandmother several times. My dad loves it here too."

"Helloooooooooo . . . !" It's Emily! "Well, what do you guys think?" She glides through the room in the sparkly silver gown. I gasp. I can't speak, so instead I give her two thumbs-up, followed by the Vulcan sign with both my right and left hands.

I could stare at Emily all day, but Millicent insists on a backstage tour of the theater. She has a thousand questions.

"When was this built?"

"Is that the original ceiling?"

"How much is that Wurlitzer organ worth?"

"What kind of revenue streams does this theater generate?"

"You're going to have to ask my dad the last question," I say as I lead the girls upstairs to the apartment. "Mom, Dad, this is Emily and Millicent," I tell them.

"Nice to meet you both," my father says as he shakes Millicent's hand.

"Hello." Mom stands up to greet them. "Won't you have some chips and cookies, and perhaps something to drink? We have sodas and lemonade."

Emily and Millicent both want lemonade. Even though I would rather have a Pepsi, I have lemonade too. As Mom gets the drinks, I bring the Doritos and cookies into the living room. I wish our apartment looked nicer. The coffee table is all scratched and one of the legs is secured with duct tape, and Dad's chair has stuffing coming out of the seat. The plaid couch, which has always looked ratty, seems a hundred times worse today. At least the vintage movie posters on the walls look good. There's *Roman Holiday, The Bicycle Thief,* and *Annie Hall.*

"I love your theater, Mr. and Mrs. Sandelski," Millicent says. "Is it on the National Register of Historic Places?"

My father nods. "It is, but still it doesn't have federal protection from demolition."

Millicent frowns. "It would be a pity if this theater were to go. My dad came here almost every day last summer."

"He was my best customer! We could use more guests like him."

"Mrs. Sandelski," Millicent says, "Marley showed us the organ. He says you play it."

"It's true," Mom tells her. "Our Wurlitzer has been here since 1925."

I can see Millicent studying my mother. "Are you blind?" she asks.

"Millie!" Emily gasps. "That's not a very nice thing to say."

Mom just laughs. "You're very perceptive, Millicent. Yes, I'm blind."

Emily turns bright red and clamps her hand over her mouth. Her eyes widen and she looks stricken.

"I thought so," Millicent says, nodding. "I've studied Louis Braille, but haven't mastered reading in Braille yet. I'm working on it, though."

"Well, Millicent," Mom says, "anytime you'd like to borrow some books, you're welcome to them."

"Thanks, I may do that," Millicent says. "But right now I'm wondering if you could play the Wurlitzer for us?"

Mom brightens. "Well, I don't see why not!"

Dad leads us downstairs to where the Wurlitzer stands.

"It's bigger than I thought it would be," Emily murmurs.

We are all quiet as my mother begins. Music fills the theater as she plays "Mr. Sandman." She used to play that music for me when I was little. Emily turns to me and whispers, "I wish my dad could hear this. He's a musician too. Marley, your mother is amazing."

I nod. Emily is right. My mother is amazing and so is this afternoon. I wish it would never end.

CAPTAIN'S LOG

Friendly alien was accompanied by odd but highly intelligent being. Both appeared impressed by the Transporter Room. Mission successful.

I couldn't sleep last night because 1) the Home Sciences fashion show is today, and 2) I will be parading around in a gown made of trash bags.

I doubt if Captain Kirk ever had an assignment this hard.

During P.E. Coach Martin pulls me out of the basketball game. I'm afraid he's going to yell at me. Everybody else did. When I got the basketball I threw it to the open guy. Only, he was on the opposing team.

"Sandelski," Coach Martin says, consulting his clipboard, "I timed you running yesterday. You went from the gym to all the way to the corner in less than six seconds."

I shrug. That doesn't mean anything to me.

"Sandelski, that's fast. You're fast. I think you have what it takes to be really good on the track team."

I pause. It would be great to be good at something.

"Think about it," Coach Martin says.

If anything, the Tragic Tree looks even more tragic than usual. Someone has trimmed it so that the branches are almost bare except in a couple of clumps.

"We are totally going to win the Home Sciences fashion show!" Max declares. She is so excited she barely touches her pasta.

"Is that true?" I ask Ramen. He's standing in the mud poking at his noodles. The flavor of the day is Picante Beef. Even though it's his favorite, he hardly ever eats it because it's so spicy and he has a no-liquids-during-school rule to avoid going to the bathroom.

Ramen nods, but doesn't seem too happy about it. "Yeah, it's true. We're going to win. Hey, what about you and Emily?" he coos. He's got a noodle on his face, but I don't bother to tell him.

"What about us?"

"How's your entry?" Max asks. "Not that you stand a chance against us. No one does. What will Emily be wearing?"

"A gown," I mumble, "but I'm going to be the one wearing it."

"YOU'RE WEARING A GOWN?" Ramen shouts.

"Shhhhh, YOU DON'T HAVE TO BE SO LOUD!" I shout back. I quickly glance around to see if anyone is looking at us. No one is. No one ever is. "Yeah, I'm going to wear it. So what? Big deal. Emily was the main designer, so I have to model it."

"Aaaaah," Max says as she spears a shrimp in her pasta. "It must be true love!"

"Shut up," I say. "She's just my design partner. There's nothing between us."

I hope I'm wrong. There's no one else in the universe I would wear a gown for.

By the time we get to sixth period, I'm so sweaty from nerves I think I'll drown.

"Marley," Emily says as she helps me into the gown, "would you mind blotting your face?" She hands me some tiny tissues from a Kleenex packet. I'll need more than this to save me.

I glance around the room. There are trash-bag creations everywhere. Troy and Patrick look normal wearing theirs. I'm not sure where Max and Ramen are.

The door swings wide open and Principal Haycorn struts into the room, followed by Ms. McKenna and her entire sixth-period class. I notice that the kids closest to Haycorn are holding their breath. He is particularly odorous today.

"Ah, our celebrity judges!" Mrs. Wilder announces. "Ms. McKenna and Principal Haycorn, you sit up front. Others, please try to find a place."

I panic. No one told me that there would be another class here. There's a lot of jostling as everyone squeezes into the room. This must have been what it was like at the Roman Colosseum when crowds considered it good sport to watch someone get devoured by a lion.

Finally, Mrs. Wilder takes out an old CD player and hits PLAY. "Let the competition begin!" she announces as the music starts.

One by one, Mrs. Wilder calls the teams up to the front. All the desks and chairs have been parted in the middle to create a runway. When Patrick does some sort of spacey bunny hop down the aisle, Troy announces, "Our creation is titled, 'Our Creation.' We have explored the humanity of man and the universe, and decided that we all belong in garbage bags."

Next up is a girl with braces. She spits when she speaks and Ms. McKenna has to wipe her face. "We created this ultramodern version of pajamas and a bathrobe," says the spitter. Her partner struts up and down the runway, clearly enjoying herself.

When it's our turn, Emily steps up to the podium. Even from the back of the room, I can tell she has really good posture. "Marley and I call our design, the 'Glamour Gown'!"

I'm frozen. She signals for me to walk down the aisle. I can't move. Emily keeps motioning me forward. I keep shaking my head. It was one thing for me to be a mannequin while we were designing this, but it's something completely different to flaunt it in a fashion show in front of another classroom.

"Marley," Emily hisses, "come on!" She turns toward the judges. "Excuse me, I need a moment with my model." She rushes back to me. "What's going on, Marley? Are you okay? You look pale."

"I can't move," I say through gritted teeth. Oh wait. I can move. My left eye has started to twitch. Lovely.

All my life I've been invisible. It even says so in the front of my lost Captain's Log. That's my word for this year. Invisible. Only now all eyes are upon me. Why? Because I am frozen in the back of Home Sciences wearing a garbage-bag gown.

"Marley," Mrs. Wilder says impatiently, "we really do need to move along."

Finally, I run up to the front of the class. My dress makes swishing noises. I almost trip on the hem. Everyone laughs. I try to hide behind Emily as she reads off an index card. "We took our inspiration from the high fashion and high glamour of Hollywood. Marley, would you step forward and show them our design?"

Instead of stepping forward, I duck under Mrs. Wilder's desk. The laughing starts up again and turns into a roar. Principal Haycorn has to yell to get everyone to quiet down. Emily lowers her head and mumbles, "Well then, I guess we're done."

"Heghlu'meH QaQ jajvam," I whisper to myself in Klingon.

Translation: *Today is a good day to die.*

CAPTAIN'S LOG

The Alliance has disintegrated.

I slip my Captain's Log into my backpack. I'm trying to make myself invisible in the far corner of the room, behind a dressmaker's dummy. There's only one design team left to go. I wonder if I should wait or hurl myself into a Dumpster right now. I'm already dressed for it. Emily won't even look at me. Instead, she's sitting near the front with her hands folded in her lap, staring straight ahead. There's a lump of shame wedged in my throat that's growing so big, I'm sure I'm going to suffocate and die. Emily worked so hard, and not only did I embarrass myself, but I'm sure I embarrassed her too.

"Max, are you ready?" Mrs. Wilder calls out. She's wearing a dress that looks like a bathrobe. I'd like to see her wearing clothes made out of garbage bags.

I don't see Ramen anywhere. Max changes the CD and when the music begins to blast, she yells, "There is only one clear winner . . . BATMAN!"

The back door is kicked open and everyone gasps as Ramen does a flying leap into the room. He looks exactly like Batman, only smaller. The mask is perfect, the cape flows, and Max even made gloves and gave Ramen muscles where there were none before.

"This is the Batman of *The Dark Knight*, film version," Max informs the judges. You can tell by her voice that she knows how good it looks.

As Ramen/Batman struts around to the music, Ms. McKenna jumps up and starts to do what she claims is the official "Bat dance." Then, if you can believe this, Principal Haycorn and Mrs. Wilder start dancing too. It's surreal, like in *Star Trek*: *TOS*, "The Naked Time," where an alien disease contaminates the crew and everyone starts acting weird.

Once the judges have calmed down, the winning team is announced. From the way Ramen and Max are jumping up and down, you'd think they won the lottery. Everyone crowds around Ramen to admire his costume. "You make a great Batman," Troy tells him. He's still wearing his garbage bag. So is Patrick.

"That's true," Ramen says glumly. "I tried to get Max to make a Darth Vader costume, but she refused. You know how she is." They both nod in unison.

"Darth Vader has asthma," Troy comments.

Patrick slugs him.

"Ramen," Max says coyly, "you look so nice. You ought to dress like Batman every day."

"In your dreams," he replies. He winks at her and flexes his fake muscles.

Emily goes up to congratulate them. She has a lot of class. Too bad her partner was such a loser. I wouldn't be surprised if she hates me. Right now even I hate me.

I grab my backpack and duck out of the room.

The hallway is empty. When I turn a corner I hear, "Well, well, what do we have here?"

Slowly, I turn around. Great. It's the small Gorn, flanked by the other two. What are they doing out of class?

"I'm not sure what it is," the Gorn leader comments as he looks me up and down.

Suddenly, a horrible realization washes over me. I am still wearing my garbage bag gown. I take a step back. The Gorn each take a step forward. I take another step back. They take another step forward. I'm not sure how long this dance can last.

I take a few strides before starting to run. Shoot! The gown keeps tripping me up. I turn the corner, only to find them gaining on me. I feel like I'm running in a swimming pool. As I make my way down Mission Street, they do too. I can hear them panting. I dart down an alley, crouch behind a Dumpster, and try to rip the gown off. It's hard to do with so much tape on it.

"What's the matter? Don't you like your dress? It's so pretty," an ominous voice says. I jerk my head up to see the Gorn closing in on me. Their eyes sparkle with antic-ipation. I'm trapped. As I try to walk past, the middle Gorn puts his giant hand on my shoulder. "Wait a min-ute, little lady," he says. "Leaving the party so soon?"

30.

Even though I can see it coming, the first hit surprises me. I double over and grip my stomach. "You can do better than that, can't you?" I sputter as I try to hold my guts in. *Can't let them know how much it hurts. Can't let them know. Can't be weak.* Like Spock, I need to be in control of my emotions.

"What was that?" the hulking Gorn leader remarks. "Did she say something?"

"She said we could do better," the small Gorn cackles, revealing his tiny sharp teeth. He makes a fist and swings. My head snaps to the left. My jaw is throbbing. I reach to touch it. It feels wet and slippery. Is that blood on my hand? The Gorn stare at me as if waiting for me to do something. I refuse to cry, even though that's what I want to do most.

I make eye contact with the middle Gorn. "What's the matter with you?" I spit out some blood. "Scared to hit me? Are you the only one with a conscience? Come on, go ahead. Come on, hit the geek kid. Hit him. Even if you kill him, no one will notice he's missing."

He doesn't appear excited and hyped up, like his brothers do. A look that could pass for sorrow flashes in his eyes.

"Hit him," the Gorn leader orders. His voice is flat.

Panic sets in as fear threatens to consume me. I keep pushing it down. Pushing it down, like Spock. Must block it out. Hide all emotions.

The middle Gorn blinks, and when he opens his eyes, the sorrow has been replaced by a cold hard glare. He makes a fist and *BOOM*. I'm down. The other two get in some good kicks and punches until one says, "This is boring. Let's go graffiti the gas station."

I lay still for the longest time to make sure they're really gone. Maybe I'll just stay here forever. Every inch of me hurts. My knees wobble when I stand. I throw up. My jaw is throbbing. I could use Dr. "Bones" McCoy right about now. At least the trash bags I'm wearing have kept the blood and barf off my clothes. Slowly I peel the gown off, then drag myself past RadioShack, and the Dinosaur Farm, and Stout's Coffee Shop without looking up.

Dad's nowhere in sight. Good. Mom's listening to an audiobook about Paris. "Bonjour, Marley. Are you up for going to the driving range tonight?" she says when I enter the apartment.

For once I'm glad my mother can't see me. I

straighten up. My bones ache. "I have a lot of home-work," I tell her. "I have a history test."

"Okay," she says. "Another time then. Everything all right, honey?"

"Everything's great."

"Marley," Mom says, sounding stern. I hold my breath. "Where's my hug?"

I exhale. It hurts just to breathe. "Later," I say.

I head to the freezer and take out the peas to ice my eye. Then I hit the bathroom. I lock the door and turn on the water. As always, it takes forever for the shower to warm up. Stupid old pipes. Digger's dad is right. The Rialto is falling apart. So am I. After I've cleaned up, I wipe the fog off the mirror and assess the damage. My jaw is swelling up. My left eye is swollen. It's a black eye for sure. My stomach is sore and bruised. My arms are red, giv-ing way to blue, which will turn to an ugly purplish black.

I look hideous. It's true what they say about me at school. I'm such a loser.

It's almost 10:30 P.M. I'm in the Transporter Room with my *Star Trek* action figures.

"Marley," Mom says. I didn't even hear her come down. "You're awfully quiet. Is everything okay?"

When she starts to run her fingers through my hair, I wince and pull away from her. "Everything's fine," I say.

"You didn't even eat dinner. Is this about Emily?" she

asks. "She seems awfully sweet. And Millicent was nice too. Why don't you invite them over again? Maybe they'd like to watch a movie from the projection room. Or we can open up the balcony and —"

"Mom! Everything's fine, okay?" My voice rises. "I just need some time alone. Do you mind? Sheesh."

My mother turns around to leave. I can't see her face, but I can hear her hurt. "All right, Marley. I'll give you your space."

I return to my action figures. Captain Kirk is paralyzed like Christopher Pike in Season One, Episode 11, *TOS*. Even though they are under attack by the Klingon, the *Enterprise* crew doesn't fight back.

CAPTAIN'S LOG

Cornered by the Gorn. Resistance was futile. Sustained significant damage, possibly permanent.

31.

I spend the rest of the weekend avoiding my father. I can sort of hide my black eye with my hair, but there's nothing I can do about my swollen jaw.

"Marley, it's dinnertime," my mother calls out. Huh? I must have fallen asleep. "Please take this to your dad." She hands me a plate of salmon, green beans, and brown rice.

My father is thumbing through a worn-out American Film Institute magazine as the projector rolls. I keep my head down and hand him his dinner. "Thanks, son," he says. I am about to escape free and clear when Dad stops me. "Marley, hold on a minute. Come over here in the light."

As gently as my mother would, he takes my face in his hands. Dad brushes away my hair and winces when he looks at me. I turn away.

"What happened?"

"I fell down. Can I go?"

"Do you want to talk about it?"

"There's nothing to say."

"Who did this to you?"

"No one."

"Sit with me, Marley," my father says, half asking, half ordering.

For the longest time Dad just eats his dinner. I watch the movie flicker on the screen. It's *Rebel Without a Cause* starring James Dean. There are more people than usual in the audience. Even though he's been dead for decades, James Dean can still pull in a crowd.

As James Dean and his friends are being chased by bullies, my father puts down his utensils. "The scar near my eye?" he says. He's staring at the screen and at first I think he's talking to James Dean. "When I was a kid, there was this boy — his name was Karl Bricknell. He was almost two years older than everyone else in our grade, so of course, he was bigger than the rest of us — and meaner. I figured that maybe he ate barbed wire for breakfast and that set him in a permanently bad mood.

"Anyway, one day I guess I looked at him funny or something, and he decided to do something about it. I remember what he said to me. He said, 'Sandelski, I'm going to wipe those dimples off your face once and for all.' When I didn't respond he said, 'What's the matter, Sandelski, are you a chicken?' Then he made some squawking sounds and beat me to a pulp. All because he hated it when I was happy.

"He never did get rid of my dimples, but he left me with my scar — a parting gift that I can't exchange or return."

James Dean is running around an old mansion. The bad guys and the cops are outside and he's trying to protect his friends.

"Did Karl get in trouble?" I ask.

My father laughs, but it sounds forced. "He didn't have to get in trouble," he says. "He was trouble."

"So what happened after that?"

Dad is quiet and I'm not sure if he heard me. James Dean is still on the run.

"Nothing," Dad finally says.

"Did he beat you up again?"

"Yes, a couple more times. I wish I had the courage to tell him to leave me alone, but I didn't."

"Did Grandma and Grandpa know what was happening?"

My father turns away from me. "If they did, they didn't say anything. We were all good at pretending. Instead, I kept my head down thinking that if I couldn't see Karl, he couldn't see me. It wasn't until a few years later that I ran into your mother — literally. She taught me to look up again." My father stops and stares out at the screen. A shot is fired as James Dean's friend confronts the cops.

Dad continues, "Marley, do you want to tell me who did this to you?"

I shake my head.

"All right, son. But if it happens again, we have to do something about it. Do you understand?"

I nod. "Don't tell Mom, okay?"

He lets out a deep sigh. I can see his eyes go from my swollen jaw up to my black eye. "Okay. There's no point in getting her all worked up."

"Thanks, Dad," I tell him.

I may not be able to protect myself, but at least I can protect my mother. Because knowing that I am hurt would kill her.

CAPTAIN'S LOG

Disclosed injuries to supervisor who had seen similar battle in earlier years. Agreed to keep extent of damage confidential so as not to concern commanding officer.

On Monday, I keep my head down. My jaw still hurts, especially when I laugh. Luckily for me, I don't laugh much. In my pocket is my action figure of Dr. Leonard McCoy, a.k.a. Bones. If the Gorn decide to beat me up again, Bones will come in handy.

"Okay, that's it! We have to go to Principal Haycorn!" Max is livid. It's lunchtime and she hasn't even taken a bite of her teriyaki chicken. Instead, she's chewing me out, like I had a choice about getting beat up.

"Marley, you've always looked ugly," Ramen notes as he studies my face in the sunlight, "but now it's worse, if that's even possible."

I glare at Ramen and point to my black eye. "This could have been yours!"

Ramen quiets down and twirls his noodles with his plastic fork. We both know I'm right.

Other than Max and Ramen, no one has mentioned my

injuries. I guess that's the benefit of being invisible — no one can see that you're in pain.

"If you don't tell someone about them, then I will," Max threatens. "We can't let them get away with this."

"Do you know what they do to people who squeal?" I ask. "They kill them."

Ramen nods. "They'll make it look like it was a boating accident or a suicide."

I nibble on my tuna salad sandwich. It hurts when I chew. This morning, my mother gave me a really tight good-bye hug. It was so painful I had to do everything I could to keep from screaming.

"Look at him. He's all beat up," Max insists. I can hear the anger in her voice. "We can't just pretend this didn't happen!"

"SHUT UP!" I shout, startling everyone, including myself. My fists are clenched as I glare at Max. "I don't want you to tell anyone. This is a Kobayashi Maru! Don't you get it? It's a Kobayashi Maru!"

As I pace, Max asks Ramen, "What's a Kobayashi Maru?"

"It's a stupid *Star Trek* test where there's a no-win situation," he explains. "It was designed so that the *Trek* dudes could experience fear in the face of death."

Max comes over to me. "We can beat it, Marley, Kobayashi Maru or not . . ."

The more she babbles, the tighter I clench my fists.

Finally, the anger rises up from the pit of my stomach and I cut her off. "This is my business, not yours. Quit telling me what to do! Who do you think you are?"

Max looks shocked. She blinks as if holding back tears. "Sure, Marley, we'll do it your way. It's just that . . . that . . . I'm your friend."

"Thanks," I tell her. I walk away quickly. I'm not used to someone at school caring about what happens to me.

By the time sixth period rolls around, I'm ready to go home. Mr. Jiang is due back today, so it means no more Emily Ebers. Not that she's ever going to speak to me again. Every part of me hurts, especially my heart. I can't believe how much I let her down. I've heard a couple people whisper in the hallway, "That's the boy who wore a dress."

Troy is sitting at his desk picking a lock as he debates the outcome of a battle between Jawas and Ferengi with Patrick, when Mr. Jiang strolls into class. "Hello, AV clubbers!" he bellows.

"Mr. Jiang!" we cry as we crowd around him. He looks like he's lost weight. The only one who stands back is Max.

"It's going to take more than a burst appendix to get rid of me! Hey, give the man some room to breathe."

We step back as he walks toward Max. She's got her head down and is punching the keys on the old Amiga computer that Mr. Jiang keeps around for kicks. "Max," he says softly. She looks up. "Thank you."

There is silence. I can see Max's lower lip quiver.

"Anytime," she answers.

"I wanted you to be the first to see this," Mr. Jiang says, handing her a glass jar with something floating inside. She looks confused. "It's my appendix," he explains.

Max stares at it before breaking into a huge grin. "Totally cool!" she says.

We crowd around her. It looks like something a dog might cough up.

"Okay then!" Mr. Jiang says, taking his appendix back and setting it on his desk among the replacement keyboards, wires, and other spare parts. "Let's get to work. We have a PTA meeting Wednesday night. Whose turn is it for PTA duty?" Everyone looks at each other. "Marley?" Mr. Jiang says. "I think it's you this time. Seven P.M. in the library."

I zone out for the rest of AV Club. I just want to get to my Transporter Room. I wonder if the Gorn will be waiting for me after school to finish me off. I reach into my pocket to make sure my Bones action figure is still there. When I find him, I grip hard. The more I think about the Gorn, the tighter I grip.

The bell rings. "Marley," Mr. Jiang calls out. "Please stay. I want to talk to you about the PTA meeting." He waits until the door closes.

I take my hand out of my pocket. When I unclench my fingers from Bones, his shape has left an indentation in my hand.

"What happened to your face? Don't tell me you had an operation too. Maybe those bruises are from a face-lift?"

I start to laugh, but it hurts.

Mr. Jiang gets serious. "Are you in trouble, Marley?"

I shake my head.

"Is everything all right at home?"

I nod.

"You didn't have an accident, did you?"

I shake my head again.

Mr. Jiang looks pained. "Okay, well, if you ever want to talk, I'm here."

"Thanks, Mr. Jiang," I say. "It's good to have you back. I'm glad you're okay."

CAPTAIN'S LOG

After a stint in sick bay, our chief engineer has returned. His physical appearance has been altered, but his heart is as strong as ever.

33.

Breakfast tastes bland. I sprinkle more sugar on my oatmeal, but zilch. Nothing. When Dad's not looking, I pour the entire sugar container into my bowl and push it around with my spoon. It looks like quicksand and tastes disgusting.

I dump it all into the sink.

"Take a jacket," Mom calls out as I head toward the door.

I step out of the Rialto and it looks like I've walked into Sherlock Holmes's London. It's so foggy. I zip up my sweatshirt jacket and put on the hood. There's a shadowy figure waiting for me at the corner. It's not Dr. Watson.

Digger stares at me. I wait for him to make a mean remark. Instead, he says, "I thought I saw your black eye yesterday, but your hair is so long it was hard to tell. Who did that to you?"

I just hand him the history homework and walk away.

By second period, the fog has burned away and it's back to sunny Southern California. I spot Emily in the hallway. She turns red when she sees me, then rushes in the other direction.

CAPTAIN'S LOG

Morale low.

34.

It's Wednesday night. I eat with my father in the projection booth as we watch *North by Northwest*. Dad's taught me to look for the MacGuffins in Alfred Hitchcock's films. That is, the one thing that motivates the main characters, even though that something might not be important in the end. In this case, the bad guys think that Cary Grant is someone he is not.

Just when Cary Grant's trying to escape by climbing on Abraham Lincoln's nose on Mount Rushmore, I have to take off for the PTA meeting. Before I go, I double-check to make sure I've got my Scotty action figure. He's the *Enterprise*'s resident tech guy. If I had Kirk in my pocket the other day, chances are that the Gorn wouldn't have gotten me. It's important that you select the right crew member to accompany you on each mission.

I get to the library early. It's cool being at school at night when the place is empty. There's no one here who can hurt me. I set up the DVD player and the microphone. I also push the tables to the side and set up the chairs to face the screen. Technically, AV Club isn't supposed to do manual labor, but Mr. Jiang makes us do it anyway. Mr. Reisman, the janitor, moves the tables and chairs back after the meetings when he cleans up. Still, the AV person has to stay until the end to return the equipment.

The PTA members start to trickle in. It's mostly moms. My parents never come to these things. They're not joiners. I wander over to the refreshment table and help myself to punch and cookies. I wrap some extra cookies in a napkin and slip them into my pocket for later. They're chocolate chip. Suddenly, something smells bad. Is it the refreshments? I turn and discover Principal Haycorn standing next to me. It must be his stinky cologne. He snags a cupcake and eats it in three bites, then dabs his mouth with a napkin. I wonder if he'll remember me from when I didn't have a hall pass.

He holds out his hand. I hold my breath. "I'm Principal Haycorn, and you are . . . ?"

"Marley Sandelski, sir. From AV Club, er, Technical Sciences."

"Pleased to meet you, Farley," he says.

The PTA president stands up and adjusts the fake flower on her jacket. She looks like that perky blonde lady in that teeth-whitening commercial. "If everyone can take a seat, we'll begin," she says, flashing a pearly white smile.

Parents start to fill the seats, leaving the front row empty. I stand guard at the refreshment table. These meetings are always so boring. The PTA president begins, "Tonight's topic is 'Understanding Your Middle Schooler: The Complicated and Confusing Lives of Our Precious Tweens and Teens.' As we all know, these are trying times for our youth and we must do everything we can to help pave their road to success." I try not to vomit. "But before we show an excellent short documentary," she drones on, "Principal Haycorn has something he'd like to say."

There is polite applause as Principal Haycorn makes his way to the front. He waves and nods to the parents he knows, which is all of them, so it takes a while. His bright blue bow tie matches the handkerchief poking out of his pocket. Finally, he begins. "It has come to our attention that recently one of our students was beaten up quite badly — the victim of bullies." A murmur runs across the room. I stop chewing. "An anonymous caller left a message on my voice mail. This person didn't say who it was that was attacked, but I have no reason to doubt the incident occurred. As you may or may not know, bullying is prevalent in middle school. There's social intimidation, where kids are shunned by particular cliques or made fun of, and there's physical bullying, where physical violence actually occurs."

Great. I get both. How lucky am I?

"I will be sending home a Principal's Bulletin with our students. It will include a checklist to see if your student is vulnerable to bullies. However, tonight I'd like to spend the first fifteen minutes of this meeting conducting an open forum to discuss what we can do as concerned educators and parents to prevent this."

A nervous-looking woman with cropped reddish hair asks, "Do we know who got beat up?"

Principal Haycorn shakes his head. "No, the caller didn't say, and even if I did know, I wouldn't be at liberty to reveal that."

"Does this happen often here?" A bald man with a fancy mustache glares at Principal Haycorn and bellows, "We don't pay good tax dollars to send our children into a den of violence."

"I will admit that, like at any school, bullying does exist," Principal Haycorn says apologetically. "But you have my word that physical violence is something that we will not tolerate. Now, I'm looking for suggestions from all of you. Our next PTA meeting will be totally devoted to this subject, but I didn't want to wait to address this."

"Well," begins a skinny lady near the front, "clearly, the child who was beat up must be on the edges of the social stratosphere. He, or she, probably doesn't have any friends and an even worse home life. A professional victim, perhaps." She looks around and explains, "I studied psychology in grad school."

My face burns as I stare at her chipmunk teeth. How dare she say that about me? About my family? That lady doesn't even know me. I look down and uncurl my fist. I've smashed a cookie and all that's left are crumbs.

Principal Haycorn nods. "I'd like to hear some suggestions about what we can do so this doesn't happen again. Anyone?"

The bald mustache man stands again. "I think we ought to have focus groups with some of the kids and hear from them directly. Find out what and who frightens them and why." Several parents nod.

Oh, right. Like anyone is going to sit around and admit they are scared in front of a bunch of other kids and parents.

"How about we create a slogan," a mom suggests. Her voice is high-pitched and she's dressed like a kid in torn jeans and a Mongo Bongo T-shirt. "Like, 'Beat the Bullies' —"

"Dumb idea. That sounds too violent," another parent says, cutting her off. "How about something more positive like, 'Be a buddy, not a bully'?"

"Oh! I like that," a female voice in the back adds as an appreciative murmur runs through the room.

"I know," the psychology lady chimes in. "We can have the slogan made into those rubber bracelets the kids like so much! That way, we can empower our children and remind them of the importance of interactive friendships."

That has to be the lamest idea I have ever heard. Like a bracelet will stop a bully. What would I do? Explain to the Gorn, "You can't hit me, I'm wearing a bracelet. Be a buddy, not a bully!"

What we really need to do is arm ourselves with *Star Trek* phasers.

The PTA president stands up and announces, "This a great project for the PTA!"

Instantly, everyone is talking at once. Principal Haycorn is beaming. "Okay, we'll have a follow-up meeting about the bracelets and form a committee, but in the meantime, on to our film. Where is our AV student? Farley, where are you?" He looks around the room. I step out from behind a bookcase. "Ah, there you are, Farley. Would you mind turning on the movie for us?"

As I walk up to the DVD player, all around me parents are still talking about bullies. I can hear them trying to guess who was beat up.

CAPTAIN'S LOG

A double cross has occurred. I have a suspect in mind.

The few times I've seen Emily at school, she's made it a point to avoid me. For now, the beastly Gorn are laying low. The only one who goes out of their way to see me is Digger. Twice a week. Tuesdays and Thursdays.

Halloween is coming up. It's a big deal at the Rialto. We have a midnight show and Mom plays spooky music on the Wurlitzer. This year's film is *Ghostbusters*. At school there's a costume contest. The winner gets a pizza party for their homeroom.

"What are you going as?" Max asks. She's wearing another new Batman T-shirt.

I'm sure it was Max who made that phone call to Haycorn, but she's acting like nothing happened. If she can play that game, so can I. It occurred to me that it could also have been Mr. Min, Officer Ramsey, Mr. Jiang, Ramen, or my father. But I'm fairly certain it was Max since she's been so vocal about it.

"I'm not going to wear a costume," I tell her. "It's stupid."

"Well, if you were going to dress up, who would you go as?" Max persists. When she gets on a subject, she just can't let go.

"Spock," I finally say. I wonder if I should at least wear my Spock ears to school. That would be kind of cool. Then I remember the time in third grade when I forgot to take them off when I got to class. The only person who didn't make fun of me was Stanford Wong, but that's because he was wearing Spock ears too.

"What about you, Ramen?" Max asks. She's eating sushi again today and he's hovering over her.

"Luke Skywalker, of course. Duh! His name's Luke. My real name is Luke. The first initial of his last name is *S* — Skywalker. The first initial of my last name is *S* — Serrano. It's like we're the exact same person. What about you?"

"I'm going as Batman," Max declares.

"You can't," Ramen tells her.

"Why not?"

"Because you're a girl."

Max points her chopsticks so that they are level with his nose. "So?"

"So?" Ramen echoes. He takes a step back so as not to get chopsticks up his nostrils. "So, Batman is a man. Bat-*man*, not Bat-seventh-grade-girl."

"Like that even matters." Max's voice starts rising. "You're going as Luke Skywalker, and you're a dweeb and he wasn't. His name is Luke Skywalker, not Luke-I-am-a-seventh-grade-dweeb!"

As they argue, I watch the other students having lunch in the courtyard. The most popular kids eat in the cafeteria. There are certain tables that are unofficially reserved for their kind, like that's even fair. I'm sure Emily sits at one of those tables. The only time I go into the cafeteria is when I'm checking on the LED board, and even then it's always during AV Club, when Mr. Reisman is mopping the floor.

Then there are the kids who eat outside. Some do it because the weather is usually really nice. Others do it to get away from the cafeteria kids. For me and Ramen, it was just a given that we'd eat outside, and that our bench would be broken, and that the Tragic Tree only gives off shade if you stand in the mud.

". . . bats hang upside down and suck blood. What kind of hero is that?"

"Luke Skywalker had a crush on his sister," Max shoots back. "How sick is that?"

"Number one," Ramen yells, his face all red, "he didn't know she was his sister, and number two, he did NOT have a crush on her. That's a myth started by anti–*Star Wars* idiots!"

As they argue, I take a bite of my turkey sandwich, and

that's when I spot her. It's Emily walking across the quad. Alone. She's wearing a navy blue dress that looks like a sailor suit. Should I say something to her? I try to muster my courage.

Emily looks startled when I tap her on the shoulder. Instantly, her face clouds with worry.

"I'm sorry," I blurt out. I can't stop fidgeting.

"For what?" She looks confused.

"For the fashion show," I say. Shouldn't she know what I'm talking about? Oh wait. How could I be so stupid? Stupid, stupid, stupid. She's probably already forgotten about me. I'll bet she doesn't even remember my name. Why would a girl like Emily Ebers even bother talking to me? Stupid.

"Marley," Emily says. "I'm the one who needs to apologize." Her eyes fill with tears. "I've felt so bad about how I treated you. Oh, Marley, I practically ruined your life!"

"jIyajbe . . ." I stammer in Klingon. "I don't understand."

"You were so nice, and I forced you to wear a garbage-bag gown. I never stopped to think how you might feel about it. Instead, I was so excited about designing it and winning the contest. You were sweet not to tell me how mean I was. And then, when everyone laughed at you, I realized how selfish I had been. It was all my fault."

Emily wipes her nose on her sleeve. I wish I had a tissue to give her. Instead, I hand her my sandwich. She takes a bite and then gives it back to me.

"Oh, Marley, I was so ashamed of my behavior," Emily confesses as she chews. "I couldn't even look at you. You must hate me."

Oh, but I don't. If only she knew.

"Can you ever forgive me, Marley?"

Emily Ebers is asking *me* for forgiveness?

I nod. "Sure, no hard feelings," I assure her.

"But the gown you had to wear —"

I wave my hand, "Oh that, it was nothing. Nobody bothered me about it. It was no big deal."

"Really?" Emily asks. Her tears have made some of her eyelashes stick together.

"Really."

"Then we can be friends again?"

I nod. My heart is about to burst. "Affirmative! Of course we can be friends."

She gives me a huge hug. "Oh, Marley, you're the greatest! You know, after the fashion show I was soooooo depressed. I'd listen to Lavender and she'd cheer me up, but a lot of her songs are sad too. And then I'd feel so bad."

"Who's Lavender?" I ask.

"Who's Lavender?" Emily says, laughing. "She's only got the most amazing radio show. People call her and tell her their problems and she always has the most perfect song for them!"

I nod like I know what she's talking about. I'm not that into music, unlike some kids at school who wear T-shirts with bands I've never even heard of. But this Lavender lady? I wonder if I should listen to her.

"Marley, can I ask you something?" Emily says.

I nod. "Anything," I tell her. Anything, my heart is saying.

"Is that bread on your sandwich toasted? It was sooooo good."

"Here," I say, handing it to her. "Take it, I . . . I have another one, um, back over there." I point to Ramen and Max, who aren't even trying to hide the fact that they are staring at us.

"Really?" Emily asks. I nod. "Why, thank you, Marley."

"Anytime," I tell her.

As Emily walks away with my sandwich, I feel good for the first time in weeks.

CAPTAIN'S LOG

The gravitational pull of the universe has righted itself.

36.

It's Halloween, and Harry Potters and princesses and clowns have taken over the school. At the last minute I decided to wear my Spock ears. It feels good to wear them in public. I've got both my Spock and Bones action figures with me today, just for the fun of it.

Ramen is dressed as Luke Skywalker. Again. He's wearing his old judo uniform. Even though he quit three years ago, it still fits him. Ramen was good at judo. He's really flexible and can bite his toenails. The back of his uniform reads LUKE S. for Luke Serrano, though he claims it's for Luke Skywalker. To finish off his costume, Ramen wound cloth bandages around his shoes and up his legs for boots. A workman's belt is around his waist and an empty wrapping-paper roll is tucked into it in a lame imitation of a lightsaber.

Max is wearing her award-winning Batman costume. Since she and Ramen are about the same size, it fits her well. Digger is marching around dressed as a king and even has one of those red robes with white fur on it. It looks real. I'll bet if he knew I had a throne in the Transporter Room, he'd confiscate it and claim it as his own.

"I am a bobby soxer," Ms. KcKenna explains. "This is how the kids dressed in the 1950s. See my oxford shoes and white bobby socks? And," she grins, "they played this kind of music!" With that, she turns on her CD player. "Rock Around the Clock" starts and she begins to dance. "Come on, everyone! Join me!"

A vampire and a pirate get up and bop around the room to mock her, but I can tell that Ms. McKenna can't see that. As a reward for their dancing, she gives them warm fuzzies. After homeroom, I rescue the pom-pom creatures from the trash can. I've got over two dozen of them.

During P.E. we all look the same again in our gym clothes. Well, not exactly the same. I look tall and weak. I wonder if anyone's ever used a belt to keep their gym shorts up? How is it that the other guys look so strong? Do they work out? And the girls — most of them look like they could crush me. Just their laugher alone can make me wither.

As I am waiting my turn to bat and get yelled at, Coach Martin comes up to me. "I haven't seen you running lately," he says. "An athlete needs to train every day."

"I'm not an athlete," I tell him.

"You could be," he says. Instead of his usual baseball cap, Coach Martin is wearing reindeer antlers. I hope it's because of Halloween.

"Hey, Sandelski," the pitcher yells. She's getting impatient and is stomping the mound so hard that dust is rising. "You're up!"

I go up to the plate and one . . . two . . . three.

I strike out.

See, I'm not an athlete.

At lunch, Ramen, Max, and I watch the parade of costumed middle schoolers tramping in a circle around the courtyard. Principal Haycorn is the sole judge. He's wearing jeans, a leather vest, a cowboy hat, and, inexplicably, ski boots. I see Mr. Jiang crossing the courtyard. He's wearing a suit. He wore that last year at Halloween and it cracked us all up. As expected, Digger, in his king's crown and robe, wins.

"He only won because Principal Haycorn is angling for a new admin building," Ramen growls.

"What do you mean?" asks Max as she adjusts her Batman costume. She should have won — anyone can see that. Well, anyone who would have taken the time to look.

"Money," Ramen tells her. "Digger's dad owns half the town."

I explain, "His family gives money for things like the basketball team and stuff. In exchange, their ignoramus son gets to win the costume contest."

Max and I are silent as we watch a mob of kids congratulate Digger. I guess you don't have to be likable to be popular.

The bell rings. As we throw away our trash and head to class, I catch a glimpse of an angel in white. It's Emily Ebers. As I stop and stare, Max whispers "Hey, Keebler Elves and angels aren't even in the same universe."

"I'm not an elf. I'm Mr. Spock," I correct her.

Max can be so annoying, especially when she's right.

There's actually a line to get into the midnight show at the Rialto. I'm manning the ticket booth as Mom's spooky organ music spills out onto the street. Cedra is selling candy at the concession stand and the profits go to Dial-a-Ride. Dad's in the projection booth.

"Three tickets, loser." I look up to see the Gorn. They're the scariest things I've seen all night and they're not even in costume.

"That will be twenty-four dollars," I tell the Gorn leader. His head is so big, I wonder if it's hard for him to get T-shirts on over it.

"That will be free," he tells me. "Right, Captain Kirk?"

Oh God, are they so stupid that they don't even know I am Spock? Hello? I'm wearing my Spock ears and Spock shirt.

"Twenty-four dollars," I repeat. The middle Gorn begins cracking his knuckles, while the small one takes his gum out of his mouth and sticks it on the ticket booth window.

Behind them, people are getting antsy. "Come on!" someone yells impatiently.

I can't afford this standoff any longer. I pass three tickets out the window.

The middle Gorn grins so that his smile takes over half his face. He looks like a Halloween pumpkin, only not as attractive. "Thanks, lady," he says. "You bought yourself a couple of days off."

It's after midnight. Halloween was a huge success. My parents are so happy. It isn't often the Rialto is even half full. We should have Halloween every night.

I'm in the Transporter Room. I've moved the old radio from one of the offices in here. It's covered with dust and I don't even know if it still works. I turn it on and it's all scratchy, so I take off the back and fiddle with the wires. There, it's working now. I keep turning the channels until I find what I'm looking for . . .

"Hello, all you night owls," a lady with a low soothing voice says. "Welcome to *Love Songs with Lavender.*"

Love songs? Why would Emily Ebers listen to love songs and tell me about it?

CAPTAIN'S LOG

Interplanetary mission successful despite presence of Gorn. Currently trying to decipher code by listening to emissary named Lavender.

37.

It's been a couple weeks since Halloween, and the Gorn have resumed shoving me against the lockers, only with a fury they didn't have before. Now and then, some wannabe baby Gorn will shove me too, and the bravest of the babies will go as far as to slug me. Still, their technique is not nearly as good as their role models'.

Today's wannabe baby Gorn is strolling down the hallway with his buddies. (Gorn always travel in packs.) He stops when he spots me at my locker. I try not to make eye contact, but I notice that although he's about half my height, he looks like he weighs twice at much.

"I'm going to make his life miserable," he announces. A couple of eighth-grade girls nearby look in our direction before going back to gabbing. As his buddies close in around me, the wannabe baby Gorn gets in my face.

Great. I'm the punching bag for a second generation of Gorn. May as well help them out. I shut my locker and shake my head. "Okay, go ahead. I'm ready now," I say.

"Ready for what?" the wannabe baby Gorn growls.

"Ready for you to make my life miserable. Go ahead, what's it going to be? You want to shove me? Hit me? Spit on me? Your choice. But hurry, I don't want to be late for class."

He looks at his posse. They shrug. Then the wannabe baby Gorn shoves me into my locker. The other guys laugh as they walk away. My shoulder hurts a little, but not nearly as much as how it feels when I see the girls looking at me and giggling.

At least the eighth-grade Gorn have stopped chasing me after school. However, that hasn't stopped me from running every day. Now I find that if I don't run I feel awful.

It's sixth period and there's an assembly today. This is where AV Club shines. If we do our jobs right, then no one notices all the audiovisual support. We may not be the most popular kids on campus, but we're the unsung heroes.

"Why aren't AV guys more popular?" Ramen muses as we head to the auditorium,

"I know how not to be popular," Max says.

"How?" I ask.

"Batman," she answers.

"And *Star Wars*," Ramen adds.

"And *Star Trek*," I say.

For once we are all in agreement.

When we get to the auditorium, we're all business. I'm in charge of the PA system. "Testing, one, two, three," I say into the mike onstage. Mr. Jiang gives me a thumbs-up from the AV booth up in the balcony.

Troy and Patrick are responsible for the screen and the DVD player. Max and Ramen are manning the spotlights and making them go on all the walls, ceiling, and Troy's butt whenever he turns around. "Stop goofing off and get back to work!" Mr. Jiang orders.

The auditorium is old and creaky. It reminds me of the Rialto, only it's not quite as grand. As it fills up there's the usual commotion. Kids are pushing and laughing and yelling. Teachers are in the role of sheepherders as they try to get their classes to proceed in an orderly fashion. I'm sitting in the AV booth now, so I can see everything from up here. I spot Emily waving to Stanford and his group. It figures they would know each other. I can see Stretch. Even without a spotlight, everyone is gawking at him as he looks around. When he spots Stanford and sits next to him, the girls behind them grin and nudge each other.

A few rows up, it looks like Digger's telling a joke. Kids are laughing. I'll bet it wasn't even funny. The Gorn have their arms crossed and lean against a wall until a teacher makes them sit down. I wonder what it would be like to be a triplet, or a twin, or to just have a brother, or even a sister. There are four kids in Ramen's family (he's number three), and Max is an only child, like me.

The lights dim as Principal Haycorn takes the stage. Max's spotlight hits the curtains, and for a split second I swear I see the Bat signal. How'd she do that? I blink and the spotlight is on Principal Haycorn tapping the microphone. "Is this on? Can anyone hear me?"

Duh. Of course it's on and working. Why do you think I always do a sound check?

"We have a lot to cover during this assembly," Principal Haycorn says. Today's bow tie is red. "But first a few words from Coach Martin."

Coach Martin bounds up the stairs to the stage. Instead of his usual shorts, he's wearing track pants. Now that we're into November, it's been getting cooler outside. Coach Martin takes the microphone and taps it. Why do they all do that? Will someone please tell me?

"Hello!" he bellows. I adjust the volume on his mike. "As you Tigers all know, the annual Tiggy Tiger Turkey Trot is coming up very soon. This year will be an extra-special one. That's because the father of one of our students is donating this to the school!" Some kid comes onstage hauling the biggest trophy I have ever seen. "This," Coach Martin proclaims, "is the Tiggy Tiger Turkey Trot Ronster Award! The winner will get to keep it for one year, then pass it on to the next year's winner. Isn't it a beaut? Digger, please thank your father for us!"

Digger stands and takes a bow. What a jerk.

Coach Martin exits the stage, and Principal Haycorn comes back. Tweedledee and Tweedledum.

Next, Principal Haycorn announces, "I have something very serious to talk to you all about today. It has come to my attention that Rancho Rosetta Middle School is not the paradise many of us thought it was."

Are principals always the last to know?

He continues, "Recently, we've had reports of bullying." I sit up. "Ask yourselves: Have you ever been the victim of bullying? Do you know someone who's been bullied? Perhaps you yourself are a bully. Today we have an excellent movie about bullies, how to spot them, and how to stop them. . . ."

As he rambles on I can see the students fidgeting in their seats. Those who aren't moving have fallen asleep. Even the teachers look like zombies.

". . . and so, bullying is not to be tolerated at Rancho Rosetta Middle School," Principal Haycorn says. I wonder if he ever bores himself. If he bored himself to death, would that be considered suicide? "Lights, please!" he shouts into the microphone. Ramen turns down the lights. Troy lowers the screen. Patrick starts the DVD. "And now, sit back and watch *The Bully Amongst Us*."

As the movie plays I can feel my face burn. Good thing it's dark, and I'm all alone up here in the AV booth. "Speak up," a Hispanic girl with long brown hair is saying to an Asian girl in a wheelchair. The acting is atrocious. "A counselor, a teacher, your parents. Speak up." Gee, I wonder if she was talking to Max. "Speak up," the girls in the video begin to chant.

The movie bullies — one white, one black, one brown, all afflicted with the same overacting disease — are sent to the Indian principal. On the wall is a poster of an eagle and the slogan SOAR TO SUCCEED. Principal Haycorn has that poster in his office. "Can you see the error of your ways?" the principal asks as the camera cuts to her giving a look so sincere you'd think she was talking to newborn puppies.

"Yes! Yes!" the white bully cries. His hair is too neat and his white T-shirt looks like it was ironed. "I never realized how much my negative actions affected others . . . and my well-being."

The camera moves in close as a tear drops from the bully's eye. In the end, all the pretend kids are smiling as they skip across campus. The white bully stops and looks right at the camera. The music swells. "Hey, dudes, I was wrong to be a bully. I can see that now and I know my life is going to get better starting today. Totally rad, cool, and upright . . . that's me now."

He turns to one of the Hispanic girls he bullied and holds out his hand. She takes it and then all the fake kids join hands and walk off toward the sunset together.

Right. Like anyone would believe that crap.

Ramen brings the house lights back up. Principal Haycorn appears. His arm is all red. "No, my arm didn't get attacked by bullies," he jokes. "But this does have something to do with them." He takes off a red rubber bracelet and holds it up. "Your PTA has generously created these *Be a buddy, not a bully* bracelets. We have one for each of you. The next time you see someone being bullied, be a buddy — because the next victim could be you!

"Now I want to see everyone wearing one of these. At Rancho Rosetta Middle School, we will not stand for bullying! Come on, everyone repeat after me . . ."

The audience chants, "Be a buddy, not a bully," as the teachers pass out the bracelets. Good thing I'm way up here and too far away to get one. This whole thing is making me ill.

CAPTAIN'S LOG

Communications jumbled. Message weak. Effort wasted.

38.

Even though school is dismissed, the AV Club stays behind to break down the equipment. Max rushes up to me. "Here," she says. "I got you one."

I push the bracelet away. "Why would I want that?" I ask, trying to gauge her reaction.

"I've got mine on," Ramen says, waving his wrist in front of my face. "Be a buddy, not a bully."

I ignore Ramen. "Forget it," I say to Max.

She looks disappointed. Max slips the bracelet on her wrist, so now she's wearing two. "I don't get you, Marley. Did you even watch the movie? We can bring down those bullies. All we have to do is tell someone about them."

My eyes narrow as I look at her. "Maybe someone already has," I say accusingly.

"What's that supposed to mean?"

"You tell me, Max," I answer. "You tell me."

Before she can say anything, I exit the auditorium. The Gorn are nowhere to be seen. As I walk down the hallway, it's empty except for some scattered papers on the ground and an old water bottle here and there. I turn the corner and stop cold.

"We've been waiting for you," the Gorn leader says. "Will you be my buddy?"

The three of them are standing in front of me with their arms up, like they're surrendering. Only, they're not. Instead, they are wearing a red bracelet on each arm. The bracelets look tight on their beefy wrists.

"Yes, will you be my buddy?" the small Gorn echoes as he bares his sharp teeth.

I turn to the middle Gorn, the one who gave me the black eye. "We don't want to be bullies, we want to be buddies," he says sarcastically.

"Well, guys," I say, "I don't want to be either." And with that I take off with them in hot pursuit. It looks like the race is on again.

CAPTAIN'S LOG

The Gorn have rematerialized in full force. Their mission is to destroy.

39.

It's Wednesday morning. Thanksgiving is tomorrow, plus we get Friday off too. "Well, Mr. Sandelski," Coach Martin is saying. His beloved whistle hangs around his neck. As always, he's wearing an orange Rancho Rosetta Middle School shirt with the word COACH emblazoned on it. "This afternoon is the Tiggy Tiger Turkey Trot. You game?"

I shake my head. "AV Club, I mean Technical Sciences, is videotaping the run. I need to be there for that," I explain.

"I can get you out of that," Coach Martin says. "I'll talk to Jiang."

"That's okay. But thanks anyway."

A lot of the kids are excited about the Tiggy Tiger Turkey Trot. It's a really big deal at our school. No one in AV Club is into sports, unless you count video games or battling with lasers. Besides, sports always start sixth period, same time as AV Club. Me, I still run every day, and I have to admit that I'm getting faster. Not that speed matters. What's important is that when I run, it's like I'm orbiting through space at warp speed, and no one can stop me.

Suddenly, it's sixth period and we're scrambling to get ready for the race. Our AV Club video of the Turkey Trot will be shown at the New Year's assembly on the first day back at school. "Okay!" Mr. Jiang is saying as he stretches. When he gets stuck on his third deep knee bend, Troy helps him up. "We'll work in teams. One person to video-tape, the other to run interference. Keep in mind that the race is very competitive, plus it's dangerous. Remember last year when a parent tried to take photos and got tram-pled?" Everyone but Max nods. She wasn't here last year.

Mr. Jiang continues. "Troy and Patrick, you shoot at the starting line. Once everyone is running, take off and make sure you get shots of everyone, and not just girls like last year. Ramen and Max, I want you stationed at the finish line. It's a 2K, so that means it's 1.25 miles. It will go by faster than you think. Everyone ready?"

I raise my hand. "Mr. Jiang, what about me?"

"Marley, you're my troubleshooter. I want you at the starting line and then once the race is underway, you go wherever you're needed."

There's a lot of jostling for position at the starting line. Troy sets up the camera on a tripod. "Go stand by the starting line so I can get a white balance," Patrick orders.

When I stand with the runners, I get pushed around. It's okay. I'm used to it. Just as I am about to return to Patrick and Troy, Coach Martin appears. He blows his whistle and everyone freezes. I take a step and he barks, "Sandelski, stay where you are."

"But —"

"But nothing, Sandelski. I gave you an order." Coach Martin blows his whistle again to get everyone's attention, then turns on his bullhorn. He looks natural hollering into it. I wonder if he uses one at home? At the grocery store? When he drives? I can just hear him, "Hey, you, the driver in the red Fiesta, speed it up!"

"Welcome to the 37th Annual All-School Tiggy Tiger Turkey Trot Race," Coach Martin blares. His deep voice, coupled with the high-pitched feedback he's getting, makes him sound like a droid gone haywire. I look around and see Stanford Wong and the other basketball players clumped together in their basketball uniforms. The guys from the track team, led by James Ichida, are all wearing their running shirts and shorts. The girls' volleyball team members are all in their uniforms too. I spot Julie and she looks through me.

I try to leave, but out of nowhere, there's a Gorn on my left, there's a Gorn on my right, and there's a Gorn behind me. The Gorn leader whispers, "Hey, little buddy, want to be friends?" The small Gorn laughs and the middle

Gorn cracks his knuckles as the three of them close in around me. They smell like cabbage.

I can't move.

I can't breathe.

"Runners, are you ready?" Coach Martin is saying. "Okay, on the count of three — one . . . two . . . three . . . GO!"

I have no choice but to run or get trampled. As I head out, I look for somewhere to duck out of the race, but there's no escape. Parents and kids are packed along the route around school. People wearing Tiggy Tiger Turkey Trot T-shirts motion to me and point to where I should go, where I should turn. I begin to pull away from the Gorn and the rest of the pack. Even Stanford Wong and the track team fall behind me. Suddenly, I'm alone. This is weird. People are yelling. What have I done wrong now?

I keep going. At first I feel funny that everyone is staring at me. Is it because I'm the only runner in jeans? But it feels normal. It should. I do this every day. The spectators on the sidelines blur. I can tell people are shouting, but all I can hear is the sound of my own breathing, like I'm in an echo chamber. Even though I am going fast, everything looks like it's in slow motion. Up ahead I see Ramen videotaping. Max is jumping up and down. Coach Martin's face is all contorted and he's screaming at me. He holds up his stopwatch and points to it.

I cross the finish line and keep running.

I run and run and run and don't slow down until I get to the Rialto.

I run into the building, through the lobby, and down the stairs into the Transporter Room. Then I wedge myself between two steamer trunks and slowly slide down to the floor and hug my knees.

Sweat is pouring off of me. My breathing is louder than Darth Vader's, only faster, and I can't seem to get enough air.

I can't stop shaking. My legs have turned into Jell-O.

My eyes are watering and everything is out of focus. I'm not sure what just happened, but something tells me that the earth's axis has just shifted.

CAPTAIN'S LOG

Routine tech mission unexpectedly morphed. Forced to flee and then sucked through wormhole into an intergalactic race against time and antimatter. Warp factor 8.

40.

"Marley? Marley, are you down there?"

It's Mom. I take a deep breath. "Yeah." I wish Lavender were on the radio right now. Just listening to her can calm me down.

"You've got a couple of visitors," she says from the top of the stairs. "Come on up to the apartment."

I stand up. My legs are wobbly. As I head upstairs, I wonder who would be visiting me.

"Well, there you are, Admiral Ackbar!"

It's Ramen.

"Look!" Max cries. She's beaming as she holds up a giant trophy. It's almost as big as she is.

"Why do you have that?" I ask. All of a sudden I realize how thirsty I am. "Did you win the race?"

"No, doofus," Ramen says, poking me in the chest. "*You* won the race! I accepted the trophy for you. It was cool standing there with everyone applauding. I could have stood there all day."

What? I shake my head. "But I didn't even enter —" This isn't making sense.

"Oh, yes you did," Max assures me. "We have it on tape. You were at the starting lineup. When Coach Martin counted to three, you took off with the rest of the runners. There are witnesses all up and down the route. We have video of you crossing the finish line way ahead of everyone else."

"I shot that," Ramen says, puffing up. "It's good stuff. Classic. I should be a professional cameraman. George Lucas is probably going to want to hire me. If you're nice to me, I'll put you in one of my movies."

"Why didn't you stop after you crossed the finish line?" asks Max. She looks like she's going to buckle under the weight of the trophy. On the very top is a tiger, mid-leap. "Coach Martin started running after you, but couldn't catch up."

I collapse on the couch. "I don't know," I moan. "I didn't mean to run in the race. It was an accident."

Ramen whistles and then takes the trophy out of Max's arms and hands it to me. It's heavy. "Well, that was some sort of spectacular accident then."

"I had no idea you were so fast," Max says as she glances around the apartment. She stares at the poster of *Roman Holiday* with Gregory Peck and Audrey Hepburn. For the first time I notice that with that short hair of hers, and that perky nose, she sort of looks like Audrey Hepburn. "Coach Martin says you shattered the school record," Max notes.

"Really?" I can't believe what I'm hearing.

Just then, Mom comes in with some fruit and cheese. "Is that for us?" Ramen asks. "Because I'm starving."

As Raman scarfs up all the cheese, Max says to my mother, "Mrs. Sandelski, did you know that Marley won the Tiggy Tiger Turkey Trot?"

Mom lights up. "He did what?"

"He won the Tiggy Tiger Turkey Trot," Ramen says through a mouthful of cheddar. "Is there more of this?"

"I'm Marley's friend, Maxine Cunningham. That's his trophy," Max says, pointing.

Maxine?

Ramen whispers to her, "Marley's mom is blind."

Instantly, Max turns red. "Oh, I mean. It looks beautiful. Um, it's really big and shiny —" She shakes her head and mouths to me, "I'm sorry."

"It's okay," Mom assures her. "I'm used to it. In fact, it's flattering that people assume I am sighted. Marley, will you bring the trophy to me?"

I get up off the couch and hand it to her. "Oh my, it's heavy!" Mom exclaims. She smiles as she examines the trophy. "Marley, is this yours to keep?"

"For a year," Ramen jumps in. "But then I'm sure Marley will win it again next time."

"There isn't going to be a next time," I say.

"Why not?" asks Max.

"I just . . . I don't want to race again. I didn't even know I was running a race this time. In fact, I don't think I did. It probably doesn't count if you have no clue what you're doing."

CAPTAIN'S LOG

Delivery error. Auxiliary hardware misdirected.

41.

I've set the trophy in the middle of the Transporter Room, directly under the light. It really is impressive. There are several gold columns building up to the flying Tiger. The plaque reads:

FIRST PLACE
TIGGY TIGER TURKEY TROT
RONSTER AWARD

Ramen says I have to bring it back to school on Monday to get it engraved.

I still can't believe I won. But really, I didn't. I wasn't running toward the finish line — I was running away from the Gorn. Do they give trophies to cowards? I'll return it to Coach Martin and he can give it to the real winner.

"Marley?" It's Dad. "Turkey time," he says.

I nod. I'm starving. Dad motions to my trophy. "Why don't you bring that upstairs? That way we can all enjoy it."

My mother has prepared a Thanksgiving feast. Roast turkey, corn on the cob, stuffing, baked yams topped with roasted marshmallow, and a pumpkin pie for dessert. Over dinner, I keep glancing at the trophy. It looks out of place. It's the only thing in our apartment that's shiny and new and not falling apart.

"So, Marley," Mom says as she puts an extra helping of stuffing on my plate. "I didn't even know you were entering the Tiger run."

"I didn't either," I say between bites of turkey. Dad always gives the drumsticks to me.

My parents laugh. They think I'm joking.

"I'm so proud of you," my father says. His dimples are in full force.

"Me too," my mother adds. She reaches for my hand and squeezes it. I haven't seen them this happy in a while. I can't help but smile back.

Later, as I help Mom clear the table, my father pats his stomach several times and declares, "Patrice, you are a culinary genius!" He settles into his chair and flips through the TV channels, skipping the football games, and finally settling on a *Godfather* movie marathon. My mother joins him and I retreat to the Transporter Room with Emily's *Gamma Girl*.

I can't believe how many ads for clothes and girl stuff they have in this magazine. Everyone is happy, unlike my *Star Trek* fanzines where doom and gloom are the prevailing themes. I turn to the "perfect boyfriend" article. The guy sort of looks like Stretch, only not as handsome. What is it about the magazine guy that makes girls think he's the perfect boyfriend?

The article says, "Seth takes care of his appearance. His hair is cut short the way the girls like it."

That's what girls like?

CAPTAIN'S LOG

Studied crew member manual from another planet. Uniforms and grooming code quite foreign. Further analysis required.

42.

"Here, this is for you," I say, handing Coach Martin the trophy. I'm sort of sorry that I have to give it up, but it's the honorable thing to do.

We're standing in the middle of the basketball court, just the two of us. There's still half an hour before school starts, but I didn't want to carry the trophy around with me all day. That would be weird, like the way Stanford carries his basketball with him.

"Great! I'll get it engraved with your name on it," Coach Martin says, taking it from me.

"No, no . . ." I try to explain. "It doesn't belong to me."

"Sure it does, Sandelski, you won the race. You won by a long shot. I've never seen anything like it before."

He doesn't understand. "But I didn't mean to win the race," I insist. "I didn't even mean to run in it. This belongs to someone else."

Coach Martin stares at me like I'm speaking another language. He takes off his baseball cap and scratches his head. What? Have I slipped into Klingon again?

"Listen up, Sandelski. You won fair and square." His voice is getting louder as he speaks. I feel like I'm shrinking. "You were clearly the fastest kid out there — you broke the school record! That means something. You're the winner, whether you like it or not!"

Is he mad that I won? That it was me and not one of his jocks? When I don't respond, he lets out a long sigh. His face softens. "Marley," he says. He doesn't sound mad anymore. "Son, you earned this trophy. No one's giving it to you just to be nice. That just doesn't happen in sports. You deserve this. So can you at least be gracious and accept it?"

My heart is pounding so fast I can't talk. I nod. That trophy. That giant trophy belongs to me? I've never won anything before, unless you count last year when some kids in homeroom made a list and wrote: "Marlon Sandski — Biggest Nothing."

But this trophy . . . this trophy is mine.

Later, during P.E., I prepare to get decimated in soccer. But the odd thing is, I don't get decimated. I just keep moving, I just keep running, and I'm safe. I don't touch the soccer ball, but no one touches me. No one trips me, or body slams me, or pushes me. A bruise-free P.E. period. That's a first.

After lunch, as Ramen, Max, and I head to class, I look around the school. Then it hits me. I am the fastest one here. I ran faster than anyone in the Tiggy Tiger Turkey Trot. I stand up straighter. Suddenly, I see Emily Ebers. She spots me from across the lawn and comes running over. Her hair is all fancy, like it's wrapped around her head or something. It looks nice.

"Marley!" Emily says, grabbing my arm. "Congratulations, I heard you won the race."

She's touching me.

"He broke the school record," Ramen informs her. "I was there when it happened."

Max stands off to the side.

"Well, I'm not surprised," Emily gushes. "Everyone says you were the fastest ever. Oh! I have to go!" As she takes off, she turns around and yells, "Congrats again, Marley!"

Ramen and I don't talk. We just watch her disappear into the cafeteria like Captain Kirk transporting to an unknown planet.

"What's the big deal about her?" Max asks.

"She's a girl," Ramen says, letting out a sigh.

"I'm a girl," Max reminds us.

"Not like that you aren't." Ramen sighs again.

As the two argue, I wonder about Emily Ebers. I mean, she cried when she thought she hurt my feelings, and then she hugged me. She's always smiling at me and saying hi in the halls, and she practically begged me to listen to a radio show that plays love songs. And now she made a special trip to the outskirts of school to congratulate me. Plus, she touched my arm.

Could it be possible that Emily Ebers likes me? Naw. Maybe? Emily Ebers?

All day, kids who have never noticed me before say hello as I walk down the hallway. Some even put up their hands to high-five. Even Dean Hoddin and James Ichida say hi. I wasn't prepared for this. I feel awkward at first, but after a while I'm starting to get used to it. It's nice. Really nice. Win a race, become a someone. Is that how it works?

The Gorn are nowhere to be seen after school. Maybe they heard that I won and are finally going to leave me alone. Today was a good day. One boy even said, "When we have relay races in P.E., I want to be on your team."

"*I want to be on your team.*" No one's ever said that to me before.

I could get to like this.

CAPTAIN'S LOG

Positive readings from nearby
orbiting planets.

43.

There's a big history test coming up. Ms. McKenna is letting us know about it by doing one of her infamous raps. She's making her way up and down the rows of desks, snapping her fingers like the Jets, a gang of tough guys in *West Side Story* who are really good singers and dancers, only she doesn't have their rhythm or moves.

There's a big ol' test.
You can do your best.
The night before get some rest.
Sha boom, sha boom!
Study, study a lot
About the Civil War and battles fought
And remember what I taught.
Sha boom, sha boom!

Some kids are laughing out loud. Others are frozen, like they can't believe what they are hearing. Digger looks at me and smirks.

I know that I can totally ace the test. Plus, McKenna says there will be bonus questions, so there's a chance I may do even better than 100%.

The next morning, Digger is waiting for me at the corner. It looks like he has a cigarette dangling from his mouth, but when I get up close I can see it's just a Tootsie Pop. I hand him the homework. "I didn't know you were a runner," he says. "How come no one's ever heard of you?"

I just shrug.

"Listen, I'm going to get McKenna to change our seats. I'll fix it so I'm next to you."

"Why?"

"The test?" he says, looking at me like I've morphed into a neural parasite. "The big test?"

A car backfires, startling me. Digger doesn't even blink.

"What about the test?" I ask.

"I'm going to copy off your test," he says matter-of-factly. "So you'd better study. We want to do well."

I feel my jaw tense. "What if I don't want you to do that?"

"This is not about what you want." Digger looks down the street at the Rialto, then bites into his Tootsie Pop.

"Hey, is there a decent movie theater around here? It sure would be nice if there was one, instead of a crumbling theater, don't you think? I wonder if I should have a talk with my father."

I say nothing as he crosses the street.

The rest of the day is business as usual. Ramen and Max argue. Coach Martin bugs me to join the track team. Ms. McKenna acts weird. Ms. Klein discusses the importance of plot. As Mr. Jiang talks routers, I check out everyone's hair. Ramen looks like a Wookiee with his big, brown bushy hair. Max looks like a boy with her short black hair. Troy's hair looks like one of those magazine pictures, only of a girl. Patrick wears dreadlocks that make him look cool, even if he is into *Star Wars*. And Mr. Jiang doesn't have a whole lot of hair at all.

Then there's my hair. It is getting really long, and it really bugs my mom that it covers my face. Plus in *Gamma Girl* magazine, none of the guys' hair is as scraggly as mine. Maybe it's time for a haircut.

CAPTAIN'S LOG

Contemplating reconfiguration.

44.

"Hello, Marley!" Mimi says, smiling as I walk into Salon Ferrante. "I haven't seen you running all week."

"I, uh, I don't run every day," I tell her. Her gold lipstick is very distracting. "Um, can I get a haircut?"

"Of course!" she says. Her high heels click in the floor as she walks toward me. She's dressed all fancy, like the models in *Gamma Girl.* "I was hoping you would ask me someday."

My mother usually cuts my hair. I know that sounds weird, but she knows what she's doing. Mom has always said that if I ever wanted a professional haircut, she'd give me the money. I know it's expensive here, but, well, I want to look good . . . for Emily. That's why I'm at Salon Ferrante.

"How much is a haircut?" I ask.

"How much do you have?" Mimi asks. I take out $30 from my pocket and show her. "What a coincidence —

that's exactly what a cut costs here!" I notice that there's a small sign on the desk, and it says that haircuts start at $40. Mimi sees me eyeing the sign and explains, "Today we're having a ten-dollars-off special." She sits me in a chair and says, "What's it going to be?"

I show her the *Gamma Girl*. Mimi studies the photo of Seth the Perfect Boyfriend. "You'd look good with that cut." She runs her hands through my hair. "You may need a light body perm though," she tells me.

"What's that?"

"It's a chemical treatment that will give your hair more oomph," Mimi explains.

"I don't want oomph," I protest. "I just want a haircut."

"Do you want to look like that boy in the picture?" she asks. I nod. "Then, Marley, you're going to need a little oomph. But don't worry, oomph won't cost you anything extra."

Oh man, this perm is the smelliest thing ever. I am sitting in the chair with curlers in my hair and a stink all around me from the chemicals when I spot . . . oh no! Stanford Wong is strolling by dribbling a basketball. He stops and looks in the window. For a moment our eyes lock. Mimi waves to him and he rushes away.

By the time she gets the curlers out and washes my hair, I'm ready to leave. But she's not finished with me yet.

As she brandishes her scissors I watch the tufts of my hair float down to the floor.

Finally, Mimi is done. She circles around me and grins. "Marley, are you ready to see your new look?" I give a weak nod even though I'm not sure I want to see this. There is so much of my hair on the floor that I wonder if there is any left on my head.

Slowly, Mimi swivels my chair around until I am facing the mirror. "Okay, open your eyes," she says.

I make a strangled sound. Is that really me? I don't believe it. Is that really me? My hair is so much shorter. It looks sort of thick and wavy and stands up where it's supposed to, like Seth the Perfect Boyfriend's hair. It doesn't look like me. Is that really me? I wonder if Emily will like it.

When I get home, my father is wiping down the concession-stand counter. He smiles broadly. "Looking good! Go let your mother know you're home," he says. "She's going to want to know about your movie-star haircut."

I try not to grin, but all the way home I kept looking at my reflection in store windows and admiring my hair. It does look good. It doesn't look like me.

Mom's doing yoga in the living room. "Marley?" she asks. "Did you get that haircut?"

"Yes," I tell her. I know she's going to want to feel it, so I sit down next to her. She runs her hands through my hair and smiles. "I like it," she says, giving me a hug. "It's so nice. It shows off your handsome face."

I push her hand away. "Aw, Mom."

Even though I'm not a big fan of Brussels sprouts, dinner tasted especially good tonight. As I work on my model of the USS *Enterprise*, I listen to Lavender on the radio. A man has called in and is saying, "I just met her but I feel like we've known each other forever. So far, we're just friends, but in my heart I know that she's the one for me."

"That's wonderful, Brian," Lavender tells him. "It's about time we started listening more to our hearts than our minds, don't you think? And just for you, Brian, I've got a special song. It's by REO Speedwagon and called 'Can't Fight This Feeling' . . ."

"Who did that to you?" Ramen asks as he examines my head the next day. "It looks like a wig. Is it a wig? It's a wig, isn't it? Your hair's never been fluffy before. It's usually flat and greasy."

"Stop it!" I slap Ramen's hand as he tugs on my hair.

"You don't look like you," he says, frowning. "Who are you trying to be?"

"I'm not trying to be anyone," I snap back.

"Well, maybe that's your problem," Ramen says.

A couple of girls in math smile at me. Is it a fluke? Is it the new haircut? Is it the Tiggy Tiger Turkey Trot win?

I smile back at them, and they giggle, but not in a mean way.

A guy who hangs out with Dean Hoddin points to me and says to his friend, "That kid is really fast."

No one graffitis my locker.

No one punches me.

No one makes fun of me. Well, except for AV Club members.

CAPTAIN'S LOG

On course!

45.

I stand on a chair and take down the cookie jar shaped like Captain Kirk's head from the shelf in my closet. Crumbled bills, including a couple of twenties, spill out onto my bedspread. I had been saving forever for the *Star Trek* Convention, but, well, I've got something else in mind for the money now.

Cedra pulls up in the Dial-a-Ride van. As usual, there's no one else in it. "I'm off the clock in an hour." She takes a drag on her cigarette, ignoring the PLEASE DO NOT SMOKE sign.

"So does that mean you can't take me?"

"No, just that whatever you're doing will have to be done in an hour, 'cause I got plans. Where are we going?" When I tell her, she gives me an odd look. "Okay, Mr. Sulu, let's go," she says, adding, "I like what you did to your hair. You look decent."

I hope she can't see me blushing.

The Paradise Mall is huge. We have a smaller mall in Rancho Rosetta, but everyone knows that for the really trendy stuff you have to go to Paradise. I've only been here a couple of times before. When I was in third grade, Stanford's mom took us here. I remember her buying him lots of clothes and stuff he didn't even want.

The last time I was here was with my father. We had gone to buy golf clubs for Mom. But after about ten minutes, Dad started breathing really fast and broke out in a sweat, and we had to leave. It was probably for the best anyway. Dad ended up getting the clubs at the golf course pro shop. They were the wrong size, but my mom exchanged them. My mother is not a Paradise Mall kind of person either. Mom's always saying that the best gift she ever got is me. She's corny like that.

It's like another planet here. The bright lights are blinding and there appear to be mini-dramas going on in the holiday window displays. One has three mannequins wrapped in ribbons all looking at a giant stuffed cow. The massive escalators transport shoppers up and down, and strollers that look like small fire engines are stuffed with snot-nosed kids gripping balloons.

When I spot the RX59 store, I hesitate before stepping inside. Music blasts so loud that I cover my ears. It's only then that I realize I've got my Spock ears on. I take them off and slip them into my pocket where they join Captain Jean-Luc Picard. He's not from *TOS*, but I'm not a total elitist when it comes to *Star Trek*. Plus, he's French, and according to *Gamma Girl*, the French are very stylish.

A couple of girls who look like those super skinny models with giraffe legs glance at me as I stand in the doorway trying to figure out what to do. The store resembles the basement of the Rialto before I cleaned it up. It's dark, and there's an old bike hanging from the ceiling, and pool cues and junk are on the walls. This is supposed to be trendy? The girls continue talking to each other as they straighten the racks. I guess they must work here.

Since no one offers to help me, I have to navigate the store on my own. It takes me a while, but I finally find the exact shirt Seth the Perfect Boyfriend was wearing — rusty brown, short-sleeved, polo style. I choke when I see the price tag. I can't locate the jeans and ask one of the girls for help. Without saying anything, she hands me the pants and points to the dressing room. I wonder if I should call 9-1-1. She looks like she's about to die from boredom.

Once I change, I slip on a B-Man jacket and look in the mirror. Maybe I don't look like Seth the Perfect Boyfriend, but with these clothes and my new haircut, I don't look like Marley Sandelski either, which is probably a good thing.

For the longest time I stare at the clothes. I can't afford them all, and even to buy a couple of things would empty my wallet. You'd think that the jeans would be cheaper since they're ripped and full of holes. As I total up the clothes, the *Star Trek* Convention flashes before me. This is the first time in five years that it's in Los Angeles. Rumor has it that Chris Pine, Zachary Quinto, and maybe even J. J. Abrams, the director, will be there. Even I have to admit, the 2009 *Star Trek* movie was pretty great. It hinted that Spock and Uhura had a relationship when they were at the Academy.

Emily's face flashes before me. Her smile and sparkly eyes make me melt, and before I know what I'm doing, I walk out of RX59 with a new shirt and B-Man jacket.

"Marley, where were you?" Cedra's leaning against the van. She tosses her cigarette butt onto the ground and stubs it out with her the pointy part of her boot. After I tell her I am sorry for the hundredth time, Cedra sighs. "Okay, well, now I'm late, so I suppose you'll just have to come with me."

Cedra parks the van in front of Teague's Tattoo Parlor in a seedy part of town and we go inside. There are drawings lining the walls — anything you can think of, eagles, angels, movie stars, and dogs, lots of dogs. A big bald man wearing a leather vest comes out from behind a curtain of beads. His belly hangs over this belt and his beard covers half his face. He has a tattoo of a brain on the top of his head. I am trying not to freak out.

Cedra starts screaming and I bolt toward the door. That is, until she yells, "NICK!" and rushes him like a bull. He catches her and swings her around. They kiss and I turn away.

"Marley," she says as he's still carrying her, "this is my boyfriend, Nick Teague. Nick, this is Marley. His mom's that blind golfer I've told you about."

He growls at me and says to Cedra, "You're late. I penciled you in for five P.M."

Cedra turns to me and says breathlessly, "I'm getting another tattoo!"

As Cedra and Nick talk, I look around. A perfect likeness of Spock stares at me from the wall. Not that I'd ever get a tattoo, but if I did, where would I put it, I wonder? Lots of people have tattoos on their chests, but mine is so bony. I could put it on my bicep, if I had one.

Cedra settles into the barber's chair as Nick slips rubber surgical gloves over his massive hands. When he revs up the tattoo gun or whatever it's called, I'm reminded of the dentist's office. There are little cups of color on the tray next to him. Robotically, Nick shoots the tattoo gun into Cedra's ankle, like he's giving her a shot, only he keeps doing this over and over again, sometimes pausing to wipe some of the ink off her skin.

Cedra winks at me and I turn away. I can't watch. I feel like fainting. When Nick is done, Cedra holds her leg in the air and admires her new chili pepper tattoo. "Baby, you're a true artist," she coos.

Under his beard, Nick blushes.

"Don't be scared of his looks, Marley," Cedra tells me. "Nick's really a big old softy."

"What about you, kid? You got a girlfriend?" Nick asks.

"No, sir," I say.

"Well, then you should get a tattoo. Girls love tattoos. They'll be falling all over you. You want one?"

I gulp as I shake my head. "I . . . I don't think so. I'm not what you'd call the tattoo type. Plus, it looks like it hurts."

"It won't hurt," Nick assures me. "This hurts." He pulls his lower lip down and inside is a skull and crossbones tattoo. I wince. "I can give you a temporary tattoo using henna — that's a stain, sort of like paint, but it lasts longer. There's no pain, I promise."

A sly grin crosses Cedra's face. "Aw, c'mon, Marley, live a little. It might be fun to do something different, don't you think? What do you say? My treat."

CAPTAIN'S LOG

Explored alternate universe.
Strange customs. Stocked up on
necessary supplies. Later
transported to Planet Teague.
Took part in local marking ritual.
Did not want to appear rude.

46.

"A tat! You got a tattoo?" Ramen yells as we meet up in the morning at my locker. "I want one. Oh man, I want one!"

"It's not a real tattoo," I explain. It does look pretty cool. "It'll fade eventually."

"Let me see that," Max says, yanking on my hand and turning it over. "WWSD? What's that supposed to mean?"

"Lemme guess, lemme guess," Ramen says. "Weird Wacky Death Star?"

"That would be WWDS," Max corrects him.

"It stands for What Would Spock Do," I inform them as I admire the letters on the palm of my hand.

Both nod slowly. "That is pretty cool," Max concedes. "I can see getting a WWBD tattoo."

"I want a WWYD one," Ramen chirps up. "What Would Yoda Do?"

"Think of your own tattoos," I tell them. "This one's mine."

It's weird, but things are going well at school. No one has defaced my locker in a while. It's sort of odd to see it looking so blank; I hardly recognize it. No one's beating me up either. I noticed that when some of the kids say hi to me in the hallway, it's like a chain reaction, and others do too. Plus, today I saw Emily Ebers three times. She didn't see me two of those times since I was hiding, but she did see me as I was coming out of science class and, get this, she waved first!

Later, Ramen and I are heading to AV Club, when James Ichida yells from across the courtyard, "Yo, Sandelski!"

"Yo, you yo-yo!" Ramen yells back. "Yo, yo, you, you, yo, yo —"

"Stop it," I hiss as I wave to James.

"Why?" Ramen asks.

"Because you're embarrassing me. I don't want him to think we're geeks."

"But we are geeks," Ramen says. "Or have you forgotten?"

I'm in the Transporter Room and I've got my new shirt and B-Man jacket on. I haven't worn them to school yet. I want to practice wearing them at home first, you know, to get used to them. I can't remember the last time I had brand-new clothes.

This *Gamma Girl* article claims that girls love getting notes from guys — that a note can automatically ramp up a guy's cool factor by 47%. Should I write Emily telling her how I feel? Or would that be lame? It would probably be lame. I look at my WWSD tattoo and think back to *Star Trek*: *TOS*, Season One, Episode 25, "This Side of Paradise." In it, Spock experiences love. Granted, it was because he was under the influence of spores from a strange flower. Still, he later says, "For the first time in my life, I was happy."

Okay. So that's twice Spock has been shown having feelings for a girl. Maybe I should write Emily a note. I don't know. Wait, how about this? I'll write her a note and not give it to her.

I wonder if that counts?

Hi, Emily!
It's me, Marley Sandelski, your partner from Home Sciences, the one who wore the gown. I'm the boy who won the Tiggy Tiger Turkey Trot, and you congratulated me and gave me a hug. We also say hi to each other in the halls on a somewhat semi-frequent basis.
I just wanted to let you know that I think you

are really nice. Really, really nice and that I think
you are a really nice person.
   Your friend, I hope,
   Marley Sandelski, from Home Sciences for two
weeks

I reread the note about a hundred times, then add . . .

   P.S. It's possible I may like like you. Do you think
you could like like me back or would that be gross
or something? Because if it is, then never mind.

Then I take the note, fold it up, and hide it in my history book.

47.

In P.E. we're having relay races. The captains are arguing over who gets me on their team. Only this time, they all want me. When my team wins with me as the anchor, everyone cheers. I'm not sure how to react, so I raise my hand to make the Vulcan signal. When I do, my teammates high-five me.

Coach Martin asks me to join the track team again.

This time I tell him I'll think about it.

"... and so, this week's test will account for a huge portion of your history grade," Ms. McKenna explains.

Digger leans over and whispers, "I hope we do well."

At lunch Max and Ramen keep gawking at me like I'm a Ferengi, the clownlike extraterrestrials who annoy the *Star Trek* Federation.

"What?" I plead. "Somebody say something!"

"Well, clearly something weird is going on with you," Ramen says. "Weirder than normal, that is, which already has a pretty high weird factor."

"Like what?" I ask. He is so annoying.

"Like your hair," Max points out. "Plus, you're wearing mall-rat clothes. What's with that?"

I look at Max in her Batman shirt, jeans, and sneakers. She could use some sprucing up. Even though we've determined that she's a girl, she still dresses like a boy.

Ramen gets serious. "I never thought I'd ever say this, but I miss seeing you in a your stupid *Star Trek* shirts." He grabs my collar and cries, "Bro, are you going over to the Dark Side?"

I let out a long sigh. "Has it ever occurred to either of you that I just wanted to take pride in my appearance?"

Upon hearing this, Max and Ramen crack up. But when Stanford Wong approaches, both immediately stop laughing.

"Hello!" Max says to Stanford. "We have math together! Homework is hard! Do you like Batman?"

I try not to smile when Stanford replies, "Uh, I'm more into *Star Trek*."

He's almost my height, only he's way more muscular. You can tell because he's wearing a Lakers jersey, probably to show off his biceps and to let everyone know he's on the basketball team. And if that doesn't make it obvious enough, he's also carrying a basketball.

"Marley, can we talk?" Stanford asks.

"Sure," I answer. I look at my WWSD for strength, then slip my hand into my pocket.

Stanford glances at Max and Ramen, who are both just staring at him. "Um . . . alone?" he says.

"Trekkies suck!" Ramen shouts after us as Stanford and I walk over to the fountain.

"Nice B-Man jacket," Stanford tells me. "Did you get it at RX59?"

I nod. *He came all the way over to this side of the world just to tell me that? Why does he want to talk to me? Why?*

"Marley, you're probably wondering why I want to talk to you."

I shake my head. "I wasn't."

"Oh, okay," Stanford says. "Um, Coach Martin wants you to join the track team. He thinks you'd be really good on it."

"Why are you asking me?"

"I overheard Coach talking to James Ichida — he's the team captain, and when I told them that I knew you, Coach asked me to convince you. Will you join?"

"What do you think?" I'm still not sure why Stanford Wong is bothering to talk to me after all these years.

"I think he's right. Everyone knows how you broke the school record in the Tiggy Tiger Turkey Trot. That's major, Marley. I don't understand why you're not jump-ing at the chance to be on track. All the other guys had to try out. Lots of them didn't make it. You — you're being handed a spot. That's, like, unheard of. Most athletes have to work really hard to get noticed. They sacrifice."

Like you, Stanford? I want to say. What did you do to get where you are? What did you sacrifice? A friendship, maybe? Years of resentment begin to bubble up slowly. I try to push it back down.

"I . . . I'm not . . . How can I say this? Stanford, remember when we were elementary school?" He nods. "And when those kids let you play basketball with them, you changed. You turned on me. We used to be friends."

Stanford's eyes cloud over. "Think about joining the team," he says, like he hasn't heard anything I said. "It's a great way to make friends and belong. Just think about it, Marley. It could change your life. People wouldn't laugh at you anymore."

"Do you laugh at me, Stanford?"

He shakes his head. "I would never do that."

I want to believe him.

"What did he say? What did he say?" Ramen asks when I return. "What did he say?"

"Did he ask about me?" Max says. "We have math together."

"He wanted to talk about the track team," I answer.

Max looks disappointed. "Well, are you going to join?"

"Probably not, but I'm thinking about it," I say truthfully.

"If you join, you'd get popular," she muses. "And you'd eat in the cafeteria."

Ramen looks like he's about to explode. "That's right! First you get a haircut, then you change clothes. What's next, having some brain cells removed so you can lower yourself to the jock mentality? You know, you'd have to quit the AV Club since sports starts in sixth period then goes all afternoon. Before you know it, you'll forget us dorks hanging out by the broken bench and the muddy Tragic Tree."

"Who are you calling a dork?" Max says defensively. "I don't mind being called a geek, because geeks know their sci-fi and tech. But a dork? That's just another word for loser."

The three of us are quiet. Then Max says almost in a whisper, "You should do it, Marley. This is your chance to be somebody. At this school, jocks rule. You could be one of them."

"Great!" Ramen says, shoving his noodles into the trash can. "What are you doing, Max? Why are you telling him that? Don't you know? Jocks don't hang around people like us. They don't talk to Bat fans or *Star Wars* kids. They despise our kind!"

"I didn't say I'd join," I insist. "I just said I was going to think about it."

"Right," Ramen snaps. "I have one word for you . . . Lando Calrissian, *Star Wars: Episode V: The Empire Strikes Back* —"

"That's more than one word," Max points out.

"Lando gave up his friend Han Solo to Boba Fett. Yeah, you heard it, Lando was a traitor!"

"Didn't he redeem himself later?" asks Max.

Ramen ignores her. He's too busy yelling at me, "You think about it, Marley! You think about being a traitor. And then when you're hanging around the popular kids, you think about how it feels to be made fun of by them."

My face flushes. "No one said I'd be popular, and even if I was, what's so wrong with that? I sort of like it that people are nice to me and that they know I won the Tiggy Tiger Turkey Trot. Don't you think I get tired of being one of the nobodies?"

Ramen staggers backward. "So that's what you think of me? That I'm a nobody?"

Before I can apologize, he storms off.

Max is quiet, but from the way her face is all screwed up, I can tell she's thinking about something. The knot growing in my stomach threatens to consume me.

"We . . . are not . . . nobodies," she finally says. Her

voice cracks. Our eyes meet. "Not to each other. But, Marley, you need to do what's right for you. I won't hold it against you. If you have a chance to sit at the popular table, grab it. Just don't forget us, okay?"

"Okay," I whisper.

CAPTAIN'S LOG

An emissary from a distant planet was sent to discuss potential transfer. This is causing significant stress among the crew.

48.

I'm in the Transporter Room doing my homework. Now that I'm getting an A in P.E. for the first time in my life, I have a good chance of getting all A's and making the Principal's List.

I have my B-Man jacket on over my BEAM ME UP, SCOTTY shirt. I can hear one of Mom's students pounding on the piano. This one isn't half bad. My father stops by carrying two fruit smoothies. He hands me one. Mango orange banana. "I like what you've done down here," Dad says, surveying the room.

"Thanks," I reply.

We sip our smoothies in silence. Then I ask, "How's business?

"Normal. Slow."

I use my straw to poke at the smoothie that's stuck to the bottom of the cup. "Do you think it will get better?"

My father sets his cup down. "I hope so. I've got some

new ideas I want to try. If you come up with any brilliant ideas, don't keep them to yourself, okay?"

"Okay," I assure him.

"Marley," he says, "keeping the Rialto going is your mom's and my business. Your job is to take care of yourself, and to know that we are always here for you." Dad tousles my hair before he leaves, then looks at his hand. I've been using hair gel.

I open my history book and take out the letter I wrote to Emily. Should I give it to her? She smiled at me today, and —

"Marley?"

I look up. It isn't Dad.

I shove the note into my book, slam it shut, then sit on it. "What are you doing here?" I stutter.

"Your father said I would find you here," Stanford says.

From where he's standing in the doorway, I can only see his silhouette, like he's a ghost. But I'd know him anywhere.

"Okay?" I answer. This is beyond weird.

"It looks great down here. It used to be all dusty and dirty, remember?"

I nod. I remember.

Stanford paces nervously around the room like a caged animal, or a basketball player. He checks out my *Star Trek* action figures, touching each one. I try not to wince when I see him looking at all the warm fuzzies. With any luck, he'll think they're Tribbles, the furry little creatures from *TOS*.

Finally, Stanford puts down the brown paper bag he was carrying and reaches into his pocket. "I think this belongs to you," he says. "I found it on the bleachers after the Hee-Haw Game."

I grab my red Captain's Log out of his hands. "You found it?" I ask as I hold it tight. "Did you read it?"

Stanford looks away. "No," he says. "Not really. I don't know."

I can't believe that Stanford found my Captain's Log. I can't believe I got it back. I open to the last page. It reads, "Attacked by the evil Gorn. Shunned by the powerful residents of planet Mercury. Danger lurks at every turn. Prepare for the Seventh Mission."

Then I turn to the first page. There it is . . . i-n-v-i-s-i-b-l-e. Invisible. The word I wrote to describe myself.

"Wait," I say. "You mean you've had it all this time?" He nods. "Why didn't you give it back sooner? Why did you wait?" Surprise gives way to anger.

"I don't know," he mumbles. "I wasn't going to return it. Then, after our talk yesterday, I guess I figured I should. I mean, I was going to give it to you on the first day of school, but you seemed so angry, and, well, I know what you think of me."

We both turn red.

"So you did read it." My voice is flat. He must think

I'm a freak because he's in it so much. Like on the list of people I think are stuck-up. And on the list of people I think are fake. And on the list of people I hate.

Instead of answering, Stanford hands me the paper bag. "This is for you."

Cautiously, I look inside. "Why would you give this to me?" I can't believe what I'm seeing.

"That's a —" Stanford begins.

I cut him off. "I know exactly what it is . . . it's a 1988 *Star Trek: The Next Generation* Galoob Phaser with a light beam/flashlight and intensity control readout. M.I.B., Mint In Box. It was your favorite *Star Trek* thing when we were little kids."

"It's yours if you want it," Stanford says.

"Why? I don't get it."

He stops pacing. "Because I really am sorry for the way I treated you." Stanford's voice sounds strained. Good. He should be sorry. "Marley, I know you don't think much of me. And well . . . do you really think I'm an idiot and a traitor?"

My grip on the phaser is so strong that I could melt it. "You told me you didn't read the log book!"

"Well, I did, okay? So I'm a liar. I'm sorry. I am. I'm sorry."

"So this is like a bribe to get me to forgive you?"

He nods. "Yep."

"It's sort of a shallow thing to do, don't you think?"

He nods again.

I take a deep breath. Stanford looks like he's in pain and I want this to last. For years, I've dreamed of revenge. But now that it's mine, it doesn't seem as sweet as I thought it would be. In fact, I'm not really enjoying this at all.

Finally, I tell him, "You did what you had to do — even if it meant selling me out. Still, it was a rotten thing to do to a friend."

"How many times do I have to tell you I'm sorry before you forgive me?" Stanford asks.

I give it some thought. "Twenty-nine," I say, smirking. Right. Like he's really going to do it. "Twenty-nine times."

Stanford just stands there looking at me, then nods solemnly. He knows. "Twenty-nine," he says. "The number of episodes of *Star Trek: TOS*, first season."

He takes a deep breath, and to my surprise, Stanford Wong says, "I'm sorry, I'm sorry."

When he's done, he collapses into my captain's chair.

I don't believe it. He did it. The great and mighty Stanford Wong apologized to me, Marley Sandelski, twenty-nine times!

"*Now* do you accept my apology?" he asks.

"I guess I have to," I tell him. "A deal's a deal."

"Will you do something for me?" Stanford asks.

My body tenses. What if he wants me to do his homework for him, like Digger? Wait. I'll bet that's what this is all about. Stanford's never been a good student. His dad used to get mad at him all the time because of his poor grades.

"No way," I say.

"'No way,' what? I didn't even ask you anything yet."

"No way I'm doing your homework," I tell him. "That's what this is all about, isn't it? Did Digger tell you I'd do it?"

Stanford's face hardens. For a moment I'm afraid he's going to hit me. I brace myself.

"Are you doing Digger's homework?" he asks angrily. "Because I sure hope you're not. Digger is a loser."

I shrug my shoulders. "Maybe I am and maybe I'm not. What's it to you?"

"Listen, Marley." Stanford doesn't look angry anymore. He looks worried. "I don't know what's going down between you and Digger, but he's bad news. Whatever it is that he's making you do, for whatever reason, don't do it. He talks a mean game, but there's nothing there. Do you hear me? There's nothing there."

"How do you know?" I ask.

"I know," he answers. "Trust me."

I think about it, then say, "So, what was it you wanted me to do?"

"Just show up to track once. I told Coach I'd get you there."

"Why is it so important to you?"

Stanford shrugs. "I know what it feels like to be good at something. For me it's basketball. I've seen you run, Marley, and you're good. You could be the best. But you have to try."

"Okay," I say, surprising us both.

"Wow, that's great. Coach will be happy. Uh, Marley, do you want to keep the phaser?" Stanford asks. "I mean you don't have to. In fact, you probably don't want it, so if you want me to keep it, that's fine, I don't mind." He reaches for it. "I can just take it back since I'm sure it's no big deal for you and —"

"Stanford, thanks for the apologies," I tell him, adding, ". . . and for the phaser."

After he leaves, I open my Captain's Log. The one I just got back. There are several pages that are still blank. I'll fill them up before I go back to the new log book.

CAPTAIN'S LOG

Captain's Log returned
by leader from alternate
universe. Leader also delivered
peace offering, which was
accepted, and passed along
crucial information about enemy.

49.

It's sixth period. I'm where I should be. Or am I?

"Happy to have you on board," Coach says, slapping me so hard on the back that I choke on my own spit. "Team, let's welcome Marley Sandelski, with the fastest Tiggy Tiger Turkey Trot time in the history of the school!"

A couple of the guys give me hard looks, but most smile and say hi.

James Ichida walks over to me. He's about half a foot shorter than me, but everyone knows he's got speed. "Glad to have you here, Marley," he says. His voice is deep, like a grown-up's. "We could use another long-distance man."

Coach puts us through our warm-up drills — weird things like making us run backward and having us run in small steps with our knees high in the air. Then he shouts "karaoke" and all the guys run crazy, crossing one leg over the other and weaving. I can't keep up. It's like P.E., only a million times more intense. None of the other guys seem fazed. At one point I trip over my own feet. When I'm on the ground, two guys come over to help me up and no one laughs at me.

"Okay!" Coach shouts. "Let's get ready. We'll do a 400-meter. James, you set the pace. Marley, this isn't a race, so don't go all out, okay?"

We take off in a pack. I notice Ramen watching from outside the fence. When I give him a weak wave, he turns his back on me. My hand is suspended in air, until I run it through my hair like that's what I meant to do all along. What do I care about some idiot *Star Wars* fan?

Kids are playing soccer in the middle of the field. We run along the outside. I follow James and have no problem keeping up with him. It's strange running with others. Usually, I run away from people. It feels like everyone is crowding me. I can hear them breathing. I'm dying to break away, but I stay with the group.

When we finish, we gather around Coach Martin. A lot of the guys are bending over with their hands on their knees as they catch their breath. I'm not breathing hard, but I do it too. Coach begins critiquing everyone. When he gets to me, I straighten up. "Marley," he says, "your kick is all wrong. Work with me and we'll get it to where it needs to be so that you'll be killer out there when we compete."

James leans in. He's got a tiny mole above his left eyebrow. "You are going to be our supersecret weapon. If you can run as well as you did at the Turkey Trot, we'll smash the other schools into the ground."

"Yeah," Ben says as he does deep knee bends, then swings his arms around, windmill style. He's a seventh grader, like me, only he's been running competitively since the fourth grade. Everyone knows that when James goes to high school next year, Ben is in line to be team captain. "We've come close to taking the district track title, but have never won. But this is our year. I just know it. And with you on our team, we can't lose!"

I know this should make me feel good, but instead my stomach churns.

"All right," Coach is saying. "Now let's do an 800-meter. This time, I want all of you to go all out. Don't hold back. Are you ready?" We line up. A couple of guys jostle me. I can't tell if it's an accident or on purpose. "Set . . . go!"

We're off!

I'm not sure what I'm supposed to do. Coach said it was a race, but the others don't seem to be running too fast. Maybe they're pacing themselves. I decide that I'll do whatever James does. I slow down and run beside him. James and I are near the front, but there are a couple of guys ahead of us.

As we near our final lap, James picks up speed. So do I. We are closing in on the leaders. Suddenly, James pushes forward with a burst of energy. I try to do the same, only it doesn't feel right. When I'm running on my own, or even when I'm running from the Gorn, I feel good. Instead, right now, I feel panicked. Suddenly, I'm hyper-aware of my legs, my feet, my arms, every part of me. Still, I keep going, pushing myself.

James comes in first. I'm second. As the rest of the guys cross the finish line, Coach yells, "Good job, everyone! Walk it off. Keep moving."

I've been on the team for over a week now and I'm doing pretty well. We just wear T-shirts and gym shorts when we practice, but Coach says he'll get me a track uniform in time for my first meet. I have to admit, that's pretty exciting. Still, something doesn't feel right.

I love running, but I don't like racing.

I wonder what they're doing in AV Club right now?

As everyone heads back to the locker room, some of the guys say, "Good workout, Marley," and "We're going to run San Marino into the ground!"

"See you around," James tells me.

I'm surprised by how nice most of the guys are. I had always thought that all jocks were jerks.

"Marley!" Coach calls out. "Stay behind. Let's talk." He's all smiles. "You looked great out there!"

I shake my head. "I'm sorry, Coach. I don't know if I can do this."

"Well, this was your first week. It's normal to be nervous in the beginning. Ask any of the boys. But you held your own. It was a great show for someone with no training. Give it some time. You'll be one of the top jocks in no time."

"No, that's not it," I struggle to explain. "It's . . . it's just that, I don't know. It doesn't feel right. When I run on my own, it's great. It's like flying. But when I race, I feel pressured to win."

"That's understandable, Marley," Coach assures me as he writes something on his clipboard. "If you didn't feel any pressure, then I'd be worried. Winners have that in common, and they're able to channel the pressure of competition to do even better. A lot of athletes even throw up before a big game or meet. . . ."

This is supposed to make me feel better?

"Can't I be a winner without racing?" I ask.

"It's a waste of speed, Marley." Coach Martin looks up from his clipboard. "I've seen you. You were born to run."

"Being on the track team is all about winning, which means that someone would have to lose," I try to explain.

Coach Martin stares at me like I'm a space alien. Then he lets out a loud laugh. "You're an interesting kid. I gotta respect that." He takes off his baseball cap and massages his head. "Listen, Marley, I'm not going to keep begging you. I do what's best for the team. The guys need someone they can count on. If you can be there for them, great. I won't kid you. We're out to win. And yes, there will be pressure, especially at track meets. The competition is pretty fierce.

"But if your heart is not in this, don't do it. You've got to love the sport and the competition to do your best. Think about it."

As I run home from school, I try the new kick Coach taught me. He's right. It does make me go faster. Each time I push off, I can feel my muscles flexing. My mind is clear and with each stride I feel my tenseness melt away.

I run past the park and over the bridge. I run on the sidewalk that parallels the Gold Line train tracks. I run and I run. My legs are starting to get tight and sweat is dripping from my face, but I feel good. I push myself to go faster and farther.

I know they're expensive, but I think I'll ask Mom and Dad for some running shoes from Van Straaten's Sports Closet for Christmas. Real ones. I'll need them because I'm going to keep running.

CAPTAIN'S LOG

Visited Mercury. The inhabitants were surprisingly friendly. The leader offered a permanent position on their planet. After careful consideration, the offer was respectfully declined.

The Gorn still push me around, but I can outrun them as long as I'm not wearing a gown. James Ichida and I had a long talk and he's cool with my decision, even though he says he doesn't understand it. Stanford makes a point of saying hi to me in the hallway, which means that other kids do too. Emily continues to talk to me, and I'm using more English and less Klingon around her.

Mom and I are at the driving range. She's whacking ball after ball. There's a satisfying thwacking sound each time she hits one. How does she do it?

"I focus," my mother says. She's taking a break and I'm drinking my Pepsi. "I block out everything else, so it's just me and the ball."

"Hey, Mom . . ."

"Yes, Marley?"

"Are you and Dad ever going to sell the Rialto?"

She looks surprised. "Why do you ask?"

"I dunno. It's just that I know it's not doing that well."

My mother reaches for my soda and, to my surprise, she takes a sip. "That's true. I won't lie to you," she says, still holding onto my Pepsi. "But we're going to stick it out as long as we can. We're not running the theater to get rich."

"Why are you running it?" I ask.

Mom is quiet. I can hear the other golfers teeing off. Finally, she says, "We do it because . . . we love it. It's not just a building, Marley. It's a place of dreams, past and present. There's a rich history there, and we're lucky enough to be a part of it. The movies your father shows were meant to be played on the silver screen, in a setting as beautiful as the Rialto."

"But what if someone really wanted to buy the theater and then, maybe, I don't know, put up a multiplex or something?"

Mom hands the soda back and stands up. She reaches for her driver and grips it. "Your father and I have worked hard to keep the Rialto going, so the idea of someone just waltzing in and buying it is unthinkable. Marley, no one's going to take the Rialto away from us. Not without a fight anyway. Okay?"

When I don't answer, she asks again. "Okay, Marley?"

"Okay," I say.

"Good. Now, let's get back to golf."

I watch as my mother reaches into the bucket and pulls out a ball. She places it on the tee, then takes her stance before bringing the club up behind her. Mom pauses, then executes a strong smooth swing. *Thwack!* The ball sails across the driving range, arching in the sky.

It's the last week of school before winter break, which means that all the teachers are cramming exams down our throats. For McKenna's history test today, I'm going to need all the energy and inspiration I can muster. I'm half dreading it, half looking forward to it.

Digger is waiting at the corner. As always, he's wearing his Roadrunners jacket. There is no homework for me to pass to him since it's a test day. We don't bother with hellos. Instead, he launches into a speech.

"This is how it will go. You will take the test and make sure it's where I can see it. It's all multiple choice, so we don't have to worry about writing stupid essays or anything. Once you're done, you just sit there and wait. I will turn in my test first. Only then can you turn yours in. Got it?"

When I don't answer, Digger faces me. "Got it?" he growls. I look at my hand. My WWSD is fading, but I can still read it.

"We'll see," I say. Then the light turns green and I take off.

"Okay, class," Ms. McKenna is saying. She's wearing snowmen earrings and a reindeer sweater. "Now I want your tests facedown until I tell you to turn them over. But before we begin, I have one more thing to say to you . . .

> *It's the big ol' test.*
> *You can do your best.*
> *Hope you got some rest.*
> *Sha boom, sha boom!*
> *Did you study a lot?*
> *About the Civil War and battles*
>   *fought?*
> *Remember what I taught.*
> *Sha boom, sha boom!*
> *Now do your best*
> *On the test.*
> *Sha boom, sha boom!*

When Ms. McKenna finally stops rapping, she says, "Students, let's get serious. You may turn your papers over, and" — she looks at her watch — "begin."

I scan the exam. There are fifty questions. I know I can ace this. McKenna's even included bonus questions, so getting 120% correct is not out of the question. Starting at the top, I fill in the answers: B, A, C, A, D, D, B . . .

Digger clears his throat. I glance over at him. He's tapping his pencil on his desk. I cover up my test with my arm.

He coughs again, then drops his pencil. As he reaches down to pick it up, he hisses to me, "Don't be a jerk, Marley."

I look at him before returning to the test. This time, I lean back to give him a clear view of my answers.

As the hour wears on, there's the usual amount of sniffling and coughing going on in the room. Ms. McKenna sits at her desk in the front. I can only assume/hope she's playing music in her head, because she's bouncing up and down with her eyes closed. I get about halfway though the test and am feeling great. I know that I have nailed each and every question so far.

I sneak a peek at Digger. He's busy copying off my paper. I smile and continue. About half the test is left. I answer a few more questions, then stop to let Digger catch up to me. When I can tell his pencil isn't moving anymore, I stretch my arms high in the air, then cross them as I wait. And wait. While I'm waiting, I draw a sketch of Spock on the bottom corner of the test.

When Ms. McKenna announces, "You have five minutes left," I am still waiting. My Spock is looking pretty good. Several kids have already finished. I have thirty-five questions left unanswered on my paper, which means that Digger does too.

"Time's up!" Ms. McKenna says as she walks up and down the rows and collects the rest of the tests. She has on her red Converse today. "Your paper please, Digger." Ms. McKenna holds out her hand.

Digger scowls at me, then hands her his paper.

I smile at him, then hand her mine.

The next day at lunch, Digger storms over to the Tragic Tree. I guess I couldn't avoid him forever. "What was that? What kind of stupid jerk stunt was that?" Digger's face is as red as his hair. Two of his new Roadrunner goons are standing behind him with their arms crossed, scowling. They remind me of the Gorn, only without the muscles or shaved heads.

I look at the WWSD on my hand, then clench my fist.

As Digger continues to yell, Ramen's eyes grow so big they look like they're taking over half of his head. Max has stopped chewing on her dim sum.

"I had a brain fart," I say calmly. "I just blanked out and couldn't think of the rest of the answers." Digger's eyes narrow. "Really," I say. "Brain fart." I make a farting noise. "Brain fart."

"Don't mess with me, Marley," Digger says.

"Brain fart. Brain fart," I repeat. "Brain fart."

"If I don't ace history, I'm in big trouble," he warns. "And if I'm in big trouble, then you're in bigger trouble."

"Brain fart," I say. "Sorry about the brain fart."

When Digger and his guys leave, Max lights up and says, "You threw the test on purpose, just so he wouldn't pass, didn't you?"

I nod.

"Awesome!" she cries.

Ramen looks like he's dying to say something, but is holding it in. He still hasn't spoken to me since I joined track.

"But wait," Max says. "Then that means you won't pass either."

I nod. "It's worth it though, don't you think?"

Ramen, Max, and I break into huge idiotic grins. "Dude!" Ramen shouts. "You're the man! The Force is with you!!!" Then, as if he suddenly remembered something, Ramen gets all sullen again. "But it's not like you still aren't a traitor."

As Ramen heads to the library to return a book, Max says, "You did a very Batman thing!"

"Drop it, Max. Batman's a has-been," I joke. "They even had him die in the comics, didn't they?"

Max looks stricken. "Did I say something wrong?" I ask.

She shakes her head. "Batman was my dad's favorite. He loved Bruce Wayne and said that he would live forever. All my classic Batman stuff — it used to be his."

I'm not sure what I'm supposed to do. Any lingering anger I had about her telling Haycorn about me is gone. Max just keeps talking. "I know that in the comics Bruce Wayne died in the Final Crisis #6 series when Darkseid blasted him, but I refuse to believe he's really dead." Max begins to blink rapidly. She takes a huge gulp of air, then adds, "I know that he's going to return someday."

Her eyes shut, and for a moment I think she's meditating, she's so still. Then suddenly, Max starts crying. Her shoulders shake with each sob. I would almost rather have the Gorn hitting me than stand here watching Max in pain. I pat her on the head, but this doesn't seem to help.

WWSD? What would Spock do? WWKD? What would Kirk do? As I watch her cry, I feel helpless.

WWMD?

What would Marley do?

I give Max an awkward hug and let her cry into my shoulder. "It's okay," I tell her. "Batman's cool."

CAPTAIN'S LOG

Ambushed enemy. Mission accomplished. Assisted comrade in need.

51.

Hey, I've figured out how to slow down time! Just have Digger stare at you all though history class. The bell rings and I leap up to leave, but am stopped when Ms. McKenna says, "Marley, Digger, I want you to stay after class." She isn't bopping around as usual. Instead she is very still and sounds stern. Ms. McKenna is holding our history tests like they're on fire. "You both got exactly the same grade . . . D-plus. Coincidentally, you both got all the same answers, and both didn't finish the test. In fact, you stopped at the same question."

Digger and I are silent.

"I know one of you cheated off the other. What I don't know is who. Do either of you want to confess?"

We're still not talking.

"All right, then, I'm going to ask you some questions and see what you know. Who were the men on the

Committee of Five who wrote the first draft of the Declaration of Independence?"

Silence hangs in the room.

Ms. McKenna warns us, "If neither of you speaks up, you both get after-school detention, your parents will be notified, and this goes on your permanent record."

"Benjamin Franklin, John Adams, Thomas Jefferson, Robert R. Livingston," I rattle off. "And Roger Sherman."

Ms. McKenna nods. "Okay, in December 1776, Benjamin Franklin was dispatched to which country as commissioner for the United States?"

"France."

"Good, Marley. What is the famous second sentence of the Declaration of Independence?"

I stand up straight. " 'We hold these truths to be self-evident, that all men are created equal, that they are endowed by their Creator with certain inalienable Rights, that among these are Life, Liberty, and the pursuit of Happiness.' "

"Why did Washington cross the Delaware?"

"To get to the other side," Digger mutters.

Ms. McKenna ignores him and looks at me. I begin, "Washington crossed the Delaware to take Trenton. There were a bunch of Hessian mercenaries there, and they were basically bullies. They didn't care what the cause was. They were just paid to fight. They were mean and ruthless. At the Battle of Trenton, Washington captured nearly all of them, with little loss of life. It wasn't about who could beat up who, it was about avoiding too much battle. This boosted morale and was a turning point in the Revolutionary War."

Ms. McKenna is beaming. "Marley, that wasn't even on the test!" She turns to Digger. "Go directly to Principal Haycorn's office." She scrawls something on a piece of paper. "Give this to him. You, sir, have after-school detention for the rest of the week."

"Can I finish the test?" I ask Ms. McKenna. "It won't take long. I know all the answers."

"I know you do, Marley," she says. "But no, you can't retake it."

"But the only reason I didn't finish was so that Digger wouldn't get a good grade."

"I'm sorry, Marley. I really am. But you're stuck with that grade. You know, cheating can go two ways. It was wrong of Digger to copy your test, but it was also wrong of you to let him do that. However, maybe you can make up for it on your oral report next week." When I don't say anything, Ms. McKenna asks, "You are prepared for your oral report, right?"

I nod, even though I'm not ready for it. Oh sure, I'm almost done with my report about Benjamin Franklin. I know everything about him. But it's one thing to stand in the Transporter Room in full Franklin garb and expound on him, and another to get up in front of the class and give a speech. I remember what happened to me the last time I stood in front of a class.

"Are you mad at me?" Ms. McKenna asks when I don't answer right away.

That's a weird question for a teacher to ask. "No, why?"

Ms. McKenna reaches for a tissue and blows her nose. It sounds like a goose honking. "Well, because I didn't let you finish the test, and I know some students don't like me, but I'm not sure why. I go out of my way to be rad. You may not believe this," she confides, "but I used to be considered dorky when I was in school."

"Really?" I say, trying to sound surprised.

"It's true! Marley, I love teaching so much and I want to share what I've learned." Her eyes are now moist. "The American Revolution, the creation of our nation — this is the stuff of life!!!"

Ms. McKenna sinks down into her chair and blows her nose again. She looks dejected. "Maybe I should have been a dentist, like my mother and father."

As she tosses the tissue into the trash can, I try to think of something to say to cheer her up. Finally, I say, "After AV, history is my favorite subject."

"It is?"

"Well, sure. Benjamin Franklin, Washington crossing the Delaware, the Constitution, it's . . . it's like it's another place, another time, only it's real." Ms. McKenna nods.

"Maybe there's some way you could make it more real for your students than singing rap songs?"

McKenna sits up. "How, Marley? How would I do that?"

"I don't know," I confess. "But, Ms. McKenna —"

"Yes?"

"I like your class."

"Thank you, Marley. That means a lot to me. Say, would you like a warm fuzzy?"

"Sure," I say. I mean it. Then I ask, "Would you like an Officer Uhura?" I take the *Star Trek* action figure out of my pocket and hand Uhura to Ms. McKenna.

"*Star Trek?*" she asks.

I nod. "I love *Star Trek*. Space is the final frontier. Up there, anything is possible. Uhura's the USS *Enterprise*'s Chief Communications Officer."

"Thank you, Marley," Ms. McKenna says.

As I hold my warm fuzzy and Ms. McKenna holds Officer Uhura, we both smile.

"Marley, so nice of you to decide to join us," Mr. Jiang says. I hand him my late pass. "Are you just visiting, or are you back for good?"

"Back for good," I tell him. "I quit the track team."

"Ah," Mr. Jiang comments. "The allure of wobbly AV cart wheels and tangled cables beckoned you back."

"Something like that," I say. I call out to Troy and Patrick, "Hey, guys, I'm back."

They barely look up from the DVD player they've taken apart. "When were you gone?" Patrick asks.

Max gives me a grin. "Tell them what you did," she says. I blush when I remember how proud she was when I told her the news.

"I got Digger thrown into detention," I announce.

"Dude!" Troy shouts. "Gimme five!"

I look over at Ramen. I can tell he's listening. "Hey, Ramen," I start to say.

"Hey, nothing," he answers. "Oh, I mean, I'm nobody."

"Quiet, please," Mr. Jiang says as he settles in for a nap.

"Are you going to the *Star Trek* Convention?" Troy asks. He's now working his way through a giant bag of potato chips and keeps wiping his hands on his pants.

I shake my head. "Not this time. You going?" I ask.

"Heck yeah," Troy says, giving me the Vulcan sign. "I wouldn't miss it for anything!"

At the beginning of the year, I would have said the same thing. Only, there is one thing that I would miss the convention for. To look good in front of Emily Ebers. Forget Ramen. He's acting like a baby. I'm moving up in the world, and if he can't handle that, then that's his problem.

After AV Club, there is no Gorn and no Digger to torment me. I wait for Emily at her locker. My hand is in the pocket of my B-Man jacket, gripping the note. I had brought Uhura to help me here, but she's with Ms. McKenna now. I take a deep breath to build up my nerve. There she is!

"Hi, Marley!" Emily says, giving off a radiant smile. Today she's wearing a skirt and a pink fuzzy sweater.

"NuqneH!" Oops, gotta stop talking Klingon, that sounds so stupid. "Hello, Jell-O!"

"Do you have big plans for winter break?" she asks. Why is Emily asking me this? Maybe she wants to get together over break?

"Uh, no plans. Just whatever. And you?"

"I'm going to see my dad in New Jersey."

"Maj! I mean, good! That should be fun," I tell her. Should I give her the note? Emily's smiling at me again. "I've never been to New Jersey," I say. "Don't they have a lot of cows there or something? You know, Jersey cows, New *Jersey*. Moo."

Oh man, could I sound like a bigger nerd?

Emily laughs. "Cows? I don't know, Marley. Maybe. Well, I have to go meet Millicent at the library. It was nice talking to you. See you around!"

My heart is still racing even though it's been over five hours and thirty-two minutes since I've seen Emily. I wonder if she feels the same way? Lavender is talking to a woman who can't stop thinking about her fiancé. "No matter how hard I try, Orlo's always on my mind," she says.

"Hmmm . . ." Lavender ponders this and continues, "Jennifer, there's nothing wrong with that, is there?"

"I guess not," the caller says.

"Well, Jen, and for all of you out there that have a special someone they can't stop thinking about, here's the Willie Nelson classic, 'Always on My Mind' . . ."

I still have the note I wrote to Emily. Maybe it's time to be a man and give it to her.

CAPTAIN'S LOG

Must devise plan to deliver top-secret communication.

52.

As I get ready for school, I make sure to wear my Seth the Perfect Boyfriend shirt. I try combing my hair the way Mimi did at the salon. I'm never sure how much gel I'm supposed to put in it. The directions say "a dab." How much is that? I squeeze the tube twice to be sure to get enough.

Before I leave the apartment I slip on the B-Man jacket. I also put a Captain Kirk action figure in my pocket. Of all the guys on the *Enterprise*, he has the best luck with the ladies.

Today is E2 Day. Emily Ebers Day. I'm going to give her the note, for sure.

My heart races as I leave the Rialto. Just thinking about Emily is enough to wipe out all other thoughts, until . . . I stop cold when I see Digger standing on the corner. He doesn't look happy. I wonder if he is going to kill me now or wait until we're someplace less public.

"Marley Sandelski," he says in a low growl. I didn't know he knew my last name. "Not cool, Sandelski. You double-crossed me. No one does that to Digger. You'd better watch your back. Oh, and you can say 'good-bye' to the Rialto. I'm going to tell my dad that we need a multiplex. My dad will do whatever I say. You blew it big-time, loser. Big-time."

I wait at the signal and watch him cross the street. When a car rounding the corner almost hits him, Digger slams his fist down on the hood and yells at the driver. I try to swallow, but my throat is dry. What if Mom was wrong? What if Digger's dad somehow manages to get ahold of the Rialto?

By the time I get to school, I've chickened out about the note. What was I thinking, asking Emily if she likes me? How stupid is that? I'm going to die soon anyway. Digger's going to kill me, then bankrupt my parents.

All day I'm skittish. I spot the Gorn and hide around a corner. I'm on the lookout for Digger or anyone else who may want me dead. I dart from location to location, careful not to be seen, when — *BAM!*

"Sorry," I say.

"Marley?" I look up. "Hi, Marley!" Emily is standing so close to me that I can smell her hair. It reminds me of a sweeping field of delicate flowers, not that I've ever been in one. However, sometimes at the supermarket, I stick my head into the refrigerator that holds the flowers and sniff them.

It's like everyone else in the hallway has faded except for the most excellent Emily Ebers. I blink several times. Fate has brought us together. Or maybe it was Captain Kirk. That's when I notice we're standing in front of her locker.

"Are you okay? You look kind of funny," Emily says as she shifts her books from one arm to the other. Should I offer to carry them for her? "Is that a B-Man jacket?" she asks.

My voice has abandoned me, so I nod.

"I knew it!" she says. "*Gamma Girl* says all the cool boys wear those. I like what you've done to your hair too. Well, I've gotta go. Don't want to be late for class. See you around, Marley!"

I'm so happy I can barely breathe. "Eh . . . Em . . . Emi . . . Emily?" I finally manage to say. "Emily?" But she's disappeared. So has everyone else. I'm standing alone in the hall, and I know what needs to be done. My heart is racing again. I can't tell if it's because I'm happy, excited, or about to die. Digger may kill me, so what do I have to lose by letting Emily Ebers know how I feel about her? I slip the note through a slit in her locker.

All during English I can barely sit still as Ms. Klein

discusses the dangers of dangling participles. Ever since I gave her my Rialto essay, she's been encouraging my writing. She says I have a lot of important things to say.

I wonder if Emily has seen the note yet.

The bell rings and I head out. Stanford Wong is standing by the stairs talking to Stretch. "Hi!" Stanford says and waves. I turn around to see if he's talking to someone behind me.

"Hi," I answer. It's beyond cool that Stanford Wong is saying hi to me in front of everyone, and that he says hi first. Usually, people say hi to him and then he says hi back.

"You know Stretch, right?" he asks.

As Stretch and I nod to each other, I spot Emily way down at the other end of the hall. She lights up when she sees me. My breathing quickens. I'll bet she got the note!

"Marley! Marley!" Emily cries. The huge smile on her face mirrors mine. "Marley," Emily says, grabbing my arm. She smells like flowers still. "I didn't know you knew my boyfriend!"

What?

Stretch is her boyfriend?

I feel all the blood drain from my face.

"You're . . . you . . . you and him?" I say, pointing to

Stretch. He shakes his head and points to Stanford, who is looking at Emily and beaming.

"Stanford and I," Emily begins, "we're together and —"

I feel like I've been shot. This is worse than death. Before she can finish her sentence, I take off running.

CAPTAIN'S LOG

Communications error of tragic proportions. Situation critical.

53.

It's disgusting in here. I'm hiding in the boy's bathroom, the scene of a million swirlies. That's when they shove your head into the toilet and flush. Ramen got one last year and has yet to recover. Ever since then, he's stopped drinking anything until after school. "I'd rather dehydrate than go though that again," he swears.

One of the toilets has a turd floating in it. That's how I feel — like a turd.

The bell rings and the halls are suddenly quiet. I hear one last kid running to class. Finally, it sounds like I'm in the clear. I slowly open the bathroom door and peer out. It looks safe. I take off.

When I get to Emily's locker I look around to make sure no one is watching. I fish around in my pockets and pull out a paper clip. Quickly, I bend it into an R shape. I flip the combination lock over and insert the short end of the paper clip into the keyhole on the back. I grasp the top of the lock with my other hand and hold it steady. Yes! Troy's lock-picking lessons are about to pay off.

With small quick moves, I wiggle the paper clip so that it dislodges the tumblers. Suddenly, *BINGO!* The lock pops open. Just then someone puts a heavy hand on my shoulder.

"What do you think you are doing?"

I freeze and slowly turn around. I can smell him before I can see him.

Principal Haycorn is waiting for an answer. He does not look happy.

"Uh, I just need to get something."

"Really now?" he asks. "Because it looked to me like you were breaking into this locker." I gulp and shake my head. "Open the locker," he orders.

I do as I'm told.

Principal Haycorn gives me a smug smile. "Funny, this doesn't look like the kind of locker I'd think you have."

The inside of Emily's locker is an explosion of pink and purple. There are flower and butterfly stickers everywhere. On the back of the locker door is a mirror. On top of it is a photo of Stanford Wong in his basketball uniform. There's also a picture of her and Millicent Min. And there, resting on some books, is something I recognize. My note.

"Well, what do you have to say for yourself? Breaking into lockers is serious stuff."

"I wasn't breaking in," I struggle to explain. "This is my friend's locker and she asked me to get something for her."

"What?" Principal Haycorn asks. He looks at his fingernails. "What did she want?"

"Her special lucky pen," I say, glancing at a pencil holder stuck inside her locker. "That one," I tell him, reaching for a pen that's got a duck on the top of it. As he looks at it, I grab the note and slip it into my pocket.

"I think you're lying," Principal Haycorn says. "Your name's Farley, right?"

"It's Marley, sir. Marley Sandelski."

"Yes, of course. Marley, isn't that what I said?" I start to correct him, but stop myself. I'm in enough trouble already. "Come with me, Mr. Sandelski," he tells me as he slams the locker shut.

As I sit in Principal Haycorn's office, he taps the duck pen on his desk and glares at me. On his wall is a plaque from the Rotary Club proclaiming TAWSON HAYCORN, PERSON OF THE YEAR.

"I've got a crossing guard meeting after school," he says. "Otherwise, we'd get into this. But for now, you've got after-school detention for this break-in. Tomorrow we'll discuss your future . . . or lack of one." The Person of the Year's eyes narrow. "Stealing can get a student expelled. I hope you know that."

I try to swallow, but my throat is dry.

School is out and I am sitting in Mr. Glick's classroom. He's the scariest teacher on campus. Rumor has it that he once killed a kid who turned in his homework late. I got one of the few A's in his class last year, but that's because I worked harder than I ever have . . . and because I didn't want him to kill me.

Speaking of dead kids, Digger is sitting in front of me. To my left is the Gorn leader. To my right is the small Gorn, and the middle Gorn sits behind me, cracking his knuckles. Yep. I'm as good as dead. Plus, I'm going to be kicked out of school and have a prison record. But that's okay. I have nothing to live for now that I know Emily and Stanford are girlfriend/boyfriend. I can't even look forward to the *Star Trek* Convention. I blew all my money on these stupid, ugly, expensive clothes.

"Marley Sandelski," Mr. Glick barks. "I'm surprised to see you here. Welcome to detention. I do hope you will enjoy your stay."

The Gorn glance at each other and snicker.

"Listen up, you deadbeats," Mr. Glick growls. "I don't want to be here any more than you do, but I'm the unlucky teacher who has detention duty this week. So here are the rules for you newcomers — that means you, Sandelski. No talking. No eating. No nothing. You will sit and you will sit still. If you have to scratch an itch, you will ask my permission to scratch it, is that understood? What? I can't hear you! IS THAT UNDERSTOOD?"

"YES, SIR!" we all yell.

"Very nice," Mr. Glick says as he cleans his glasses. "Now, silence!"

No wonder the Gorn stopped waiting for me after school. They were here all this time.

"I'm going to kill you," Digger hisses.

"Not if we get him first," the Gorn leader says, laughing.

WWSD. WWSD.

"That is highly illogical," I say, staring at my hands folded on the desk. To make eye contact with any of them could be fatal. "To kill me would just get your detention extended."

"Well, then maybe we won't kill you, but slowly torture you," the leader whispers. He grins, showing off where his tooth is missing.

"If you lay a finger on me and get caught, you might get separated from your brothers in prison, and wouldn't that be sad?"

"Huh?" he says. "My brothers?"

"Yes, them." I point to the other two.

"We aren't brothers!" the small Gorn cries in his high-pitched voice. "We aren't even related."

All three look highly insulted.

"Sandelski!" It's Mr. Glick. Why does he always yell? "Did I hear a peep out of you? Because I think I heard a peep, which means all five of you get an extra half hour of detention. You can thank him later, boys."

I shut my mouth and lower my head. The glare from the other detainees burns through me.

Yep. Dead man. That's me.

54.

Mr. Glick barely says, "You're excused," before I bolt out of the room. There are four guys chasing me, but none of them can match my speed. I don't stop until I get to the Rialto. I rush upstairs to the safety of our apartment.

Uh-oh.

My parents are waiting for me.

They look like they've just seen Bette Davis in *Dark Victory*, this old film about a socialite who eventually loses her sight and dies. I turn around to leave when my mother says, "Marley, Principal Haycorn called. You were caught breaking into a locker? Can that be true?"

"It's not what you think," I try to explain.

"What should we think?" Dad asks. He doesn't sound angry, he sounds confused.

"There's someplace I need to be," I blurt out. That much is true. I need to be anywhere but here.

"Stay for a minute and try to explain," Dad urges.

How can I explain a lifetime of torment in a minute?

"I'm sorry, I can't do this now," I say as I run back down the stairs.

"Marley!" Mom calls after me.

I keep going out of the apartment and don't stop running until my legs won't carry me anymore. As I rest on the bridge, I watch the Gold Line train rush past, full of people going places. Some are staring out the window, others are reading, a few are talking to each other — but none are being stalked by Gorn. I don't know how much longer I can take this.

By the time I return home, it's dark. Mom's reading one of her Braille books in the living room with the lights off. Neither one of us says anything when I walk past her. I'm starving. When I open the refrigerator I find a plate of roast chicken with mashed potatoes and peas waiting for me. I grab it and retreat to the Transporter Room, and don't emerge until after midnight, when I know my parents are in bed.

Ms. McKenna is telling the class about the oral reports we're going to have to give before winter break. A bored-looking girl wearing about a thousand necklaces comes into the room and hands her a note. Ms. McKenna reads it and looks up. "Marley, please report to the principal's office."

Great. What have I done now?

"Sit down, Mr. Sandelski." Principal Haycorn motions to the chair across from his desk. I flop down and cross my arms over my chest. "You are excused from after-school detention," Haycorn tells me.

What?

"We checked with . . ." He looks at a piece of paper. "We checked with Emily Ebers, and she confirmed that she had asked you to get her Lucky Ducky Quackin' pen out of her locker."

What?

"Now, you were still tardy for class, and we don't take lightly to tardies around here, so that will remain on your permanent record. However, because that's your only infraction, and because it has come to my attention that you are the Tiggy Tiger Turkey Trot winner, you are excused from after-school detention. Any questions?"

What did Emily Ebers say? I want to ask. *Emily told you I was getting something for her?*

"No questions."

"Mr. Sandelski," Principal Haycorn says as he stands. "Even though you were cleared of this offense, I'm still going to be keeping my eye on you. I never forget a face."

I go through the rest of the day wondering why Emily would lie for me. It is highly illogical. Good thing she didn't read the note.

Kids are still saying hi to me, but with less frequency, like the sheen of winning the Tiggy Tiger Turkey Trot is wearing off. Right before AV Club, I hear someone call my name. I whip around.

It's Emily. What's happening? Who shut off my oxygen supply? This must be how Dad feels around crowds.

"Marley?" As Emily comes into focus everyone else fades away. Her purple dress makes her look like one of those models from *Gamma Girl*, only a nice one with a wide smile and sparkling eyes. I check to see if Stanford is around. He's not. Still, it hurts to look at her.

"Principal Haycorn thought you broke into my locker," Emily says in a rush. "He asked me if I told you to get my Lucky Ducky pen, and I thought you might be in trouble, so I said yes. Marley, why did you break into my locker?"

A war is going on in my stomach. Emily looks so confused.

"I had to get something," I sputter as I try to breathe. Is that wheezing sound coming from me?

"The note?" Emily asks.

I feel as though I've been shot. She knows about the note? I want to run, but I can't feel my legs. I can't feel any part of me.

"I read it, Marley, and thought it was really sweet, but well, I'm with Stanford, and . . ." As she goes on and on about Stanford, I can see her talking, but can't hear anything. When did my life get so rotten? The Gorn are out to kill me, Digger's dad will probably put the Rialto out of business, Ramen hates me, and now Emily Ebers knows I'm a complete loser.

". . . and so, I hope we can still be friends," Emily is saying. "Marley? Marley, are you okay? You look pale."

"Oh! Uh, yeah, friends. Okay. Okay, then. See you around." My legs buckle before I regain my balance and run away before she can say anything more.

"Cary, this is Lavender. What's on your mind tonight?"

"Well, um . . ." I have disguised my voice to sound like Cary Grant's. Only I'm finding it difficult to do a deep, distinct accent. "I have recently had a setback and somehow totally misread some signals."

"Oh, Cary, that's too bad," Lavender says in her soft, soothing voice. "Sometimes that does happen, though. Tell me, does your heart hurt?"

I nod. It's not just my heart. It's every part of me. "Yes," I say. My voice cracks and I pretend to cough.

"I thought so. But that means that you're alive and can feel, even though what you feel right now is pain. Cary, here's a song for you by Bonnie Tyler called 'Total Eclipse of the Heart.' . . ."

CAPTAIN'S LOG

Highly classified information intercepted. Morale hits all-time low. Darkness prevails.

55.

It's after school. Ramen is still ignoring me. At lunch, the three of us still eat together, only he pretends I'm not there, like I'm invisible. How long can this last?

I don't feel like going straight home. As I wander past RadioShack and Sweeteria, I try to shake off my humiliation, but I can't. Sure, Emily was nice enough to my face, but I'll bet the minute I turned around, she and Stanford and his buddies started making fun of me.

How could I be so stupid to think a person like Emily Ebers could ever like a person like me, Marley Sandelski? I can feel myself fading back into the nobody category. It'll probably be all over the school tomorrow. I can see it scrolling across the cafeteria LED board: SANDELSKI = LOSER.

I'm not sure what hurts worse, knowing that Emily pities me, or knowing that I am less than nothing. My jaw is tense. I hate those stupid kids who make fun of people. Why? What's the point? Why are they like that?

What have I ever done to them?

Why do they do those things to me?

Principal Haycorn hates me too. I can tell that he still thinks I'm a liar and a thief. It's bad enough when the kids think you are a loser, but when the adults give up on you . . . well, it's over, isn't it? I don't even matter, except for the amusement factor I provide.

Slam Marley into the locker.

Make fun of Marley.

Accuse Marley.

Hit Marley.

Chase Marley.

Humiliate Marley.

Beat up Marley.

"Hello, Marley."

Startled, I look up. How long have I been sitting on this park bench? Is it dusk already?

"What do you want, Digger?" I ask through gritted teeth. I hate him most of all.

"You double-crossed me," Digger says. His eyes narrow as traffic rushes past us. "You better say 'sorry.' "

Digger expects me to apologize to him?

I can feel the anger rising from my belly. I clench my fists and when I finally speak, I roar. "WHAT? What did you say? You're the slime who's been cheating off of me all this time. You're the one who owes me an apology!"

For a split second Digger looks shocked. He quickly composes himself. "Apologize to me, or else."

"Or else what?" I spit back at him.

"Or else this," he says, making a fist.

"Go ahead," I tell him. "Hit me. Hit me and you'll be the one who's sorry. Sorry that you're so stupid you can't even pass a class without cheating. That's what you are, Digger, a cheater. I wonder how your almighty dad would feel about that? Or is he too busy putting people out of business to notice?"

BAM!

I raise my hand to my jaw. It's throbbing. Digger's holding both fists up, ready to strike again.

I am about to run away, when suddenly something inside me snaps.

No. No more. I won't take this anymore.

I turn around and swing hard. I miss the first time, but land the second blow. This time it's his turn to be stunned.

"You hit me!" he cries. He touches his cheek, as if to check if it's still there.

"Yeah, and I'll do it again," I shout.

Suddenly, we're pushing and shoving and hitting. We don't land every punch, but the ones that do hurt.

I hate Digger.

I hate Digger.

I hate Digger.

I want to hurt him. I want to hurt him so bad that I don't care what happens to me. I just want to hurt him.

Suddenly, a big car screeches to a halt. Digger and I both freeze. A man storms out of the car. He looks angry. The color drains from Digger's face. He doesn't look mad anymore. Digger looks scared.

I know the man from somewhere, but I can't place him. He's got ice blue eyes and a reddish mustache. "Get over here!" he yells.

Stunned, I head toward him, until I realize he's not talking to me.

Like a robot, Digger walks toward him. The man grabs Digger's collar. "What did I tell you about fighting?" he screams. His face is less than an inch from Digger's. The man is scary . . . insane scary. That's when I recognize him. He's Ron Ronster of Ronster's Monster RVs, the guy who'll "do anything to make a deal with you!" in the television commercials.

"But Dad," Digger starts to plead. "He . . . he . . ."

"I don't care what he did. You follow my rules, do you understand?"

"But Dad —"

"What? Are you having problems remembering what I say? Well, maybe this will help."

In one move, Digger's dad pulls his arm back and makes a fist. He hits Digger so hard I can feel it. Instinctively, I put my hands over my nose, only it's not bleeding like Digger's is.

As Digger lays on the ground, his father shouts, "You can't do anything right, can you? You didn't make the basketball A-Team, your grades stink, you can't even follow directions. Don't bother coming home for dinner. I don't want to look at you!"

Digger's dad gets back into his car and takes off. He doesn't stop for the red light.

There is pain stabbing me. It feels so bad I start to stagger. I want to scream. It's not the pain from where Digger hit me. No, it's the pain I felt when Digger got hit by his father. Digger is still on the ground. He's crying. Digger Ronster is crying.

What am I supposed to do?

Slowly, I walk over to him. My fists are clenched, ready if his dad comes back. "Are you okay?" I ask as I stand over Digger.

He shakes his head yes. Digger is still crying, only no sound is coming out.

Suddenly, someone yells, "Oh my God, I don't believe it!"

I look up and see Stanford. He's with Tico and Stretch. "Marley!" Stanford shouts. "You beat up Digger?"

I start to say something, when Digger sits up. There's blood all over his face. "Yeah, so what," Digger growls. "So Marley beat me up. Who cares?"

"But — but — it wasn't —" I turn to Stanford. "I didn't —"

Digger won't let me finish. He winces in pain, then tells Stanford, "Don't ever cross Marley Sandelski or you'll be sorry."

CAPTAIN'S LOG

The planet has been turned upside down. Nothing is as it seems.

56.

Tonight I had a long talk with my parents. I told them that Principal Haycorn apologized for his mistake. Then I told them that I had broken into Emily's locker. I also told them I had been in a fight, but that the other guy looked worse than I did.

I didn't tell them who the fight was with, or who landed the fatal blow.

Mom and Dad took it pretty well. I'm grounded for two weeks, but it's not like I have anywhere to go anyway.

I can't sleep, so I'm staying up listening to Lavender and trying to figure out who turned the universe inside out.

". . . so she left me," some guy is saying. It sounds like he's sobbing. "And I can't eat, I can't sleep, I can't do anything."

"I am so sorry, Greg," Lavender says. "Heartbreak is never fun. I know you're in pain, but you'll love again someday. Until then, here's Barry Manilow's 'I Can't Smile Without You.' . . ."

It's morning. Digger is waiting for me at the corner. His nose is bandaged. He looks awful. Not that I look good.

"About yesterday," he says as soon as he sees me. "Just let people think you beat me up, okay?"

"But why? I don't understand."

Digger looks at me, only this time, there's no anger in his eyes. Only hurt. "Marley, it's a gift, okay. Let everyone think you did this." He motions to his broken nose.

"But why?"

"Because . . ." He struggles for words. This is a Digger I have never met before. ". . . because I don't want anyone to know who really hit me."

"But you can't let him —"

"Please," Digger begs. Fear flashes in his eyes. "Promise you won't tell. No one at school can know. Please."

Finally, I nod. It's only then that he relaxes. We are both silent for the longest time.

"Digger?"

"Yeah?"

"I don't want to do your homework anymore."

"Whatever you say," he says. "Whatever you want."

When the light turns green, instead of going first like he usually does, Digger waits and lets me cross first.

CAPTAIN'S LOG

The enemy is not as strong as he appears to be.

57.

Rumor of our fight has spread like wildfire. People are calling me a hero for something I didn't even do. They're happy that I supposedly beat Digger up? No one should be happy when someone gets hurt. I feel like a fraud in every way possible. I'm no hero. All I did was stand by and watch Digger get his nose broken by his father. I should have tried to stop it.

During homeroom, everyone tries not to stare at Digger and me. I fidget in my seat, but notice that Digger looks calm. Well, as calm as someone whose face is bandaged up can look. At one point he glances at me and gives me a weak smile that's so small, I don't think anyone else notices.

On my way to class Dean Hoddin stops me. "You're the kid who won the Tiggy Tiger Turkey Trot, right?" I nod. "And you beat up Digger too. Where have you been all this time?"

Right here, I want to tell him. *I've been right here — you just didn't see me.*

The rest of the day, it's the same thing. Kids pointing and whispering, only this time nobody's making fun of me. If the light on me was starting to dim after winning the race, it's back on like a huge spotlight shining wherever I go. It's so bright, I can't see. I wish I knew where the off switch was. I wish I could go back to being invisible. I wish things were back like they used to be, when I was just another geek Trekker.

It's lunchtime. I approach the broken bench where Max and Ramen are sitting. Max gives me an encouraging smile.

"Hey, Ramen," I say. He pretends not to hear me. "Listen, I quit the track team, but I'm not going to quit you or Max or the AV Club. I hope you know that. I'm sorry if I called you a nobody, because that's not true. You'll always be someone to me."

Ramen looks up and almost smiles. I do too.

"Yeah," I tell him. "You'll always be a someone who's a wussy *Star Wars* nerd who doesn't know one end of the lightsaber from the other!"

"You're the geekazoid," Ramen says. "Hey, what's the dirt on you and Digger? Spill!"

My heart races. What am I supposed to say? Just then Stanford, Tico, Stretch, and Gus venture over to our corner of the courtyard. "Man!" Tico says. "Marley, everyone's talking about what you did to Digger."

"If I hadn't seen it, I wouldn't believe it," Stanford chimes in as Max stares at Stretch.

Just then, Emily joins us. "Marley! Stanford told me what happened. I'm not for violence at all, but that Digger is a jerk. Millicent said that if she ever becomes a scientist and discovers a new disease, she's going to name it after him."

I shift my feet and look down. I've gone back to wearing my Converse knockoffs, sweatshirt jacket, and a *Star Trek* T-shirt.

"Well, see you around," Stanford says.

Max has not stopped staring at Stretch. He looks uncomfortable. "Do you like Batman?" she asks.

He nods. "Yeah, Batman's okay."

Max gasps. "So are you," she says breathlessly.

As they take off, I call out, "Emily, can I talk to you for a minute?"

"Sure, Marley, what is it?"

I go up to her and then turn around. Max and Ramen are standing right behind me. "Do you mind?" I ask. They make some lame noises, then back off.

"About that note," I begin. "Did you show it to Stanford?"

"Marley, it was the sweetest note ever. Any girl would

be lucky to have a guy like you." Then she takes my hand and squeezes it. "But it's our secret. I promise."

After Emily departs, Ramen rushes up to me. "She likes you, man, I can tell. Hey, why don't you beat up Stanford Wong? Then Emily can be your girlfriend."

"Ramen," I say.

"What?"

"Shut up."

CAPTAIN'S LOG

The light from the other planets is blinding.

After school I run, not because anyone's chasing me, but because I just feel like it. I slow down when I near Sweeteria. A mint chocolate chip cone sounds good right about now.

There's a line for ice cream. As I wait I sense someone staring at me. Slowly I turn around. It's a Gorn. The middle one. The knuckle cracker. I pay for my cone and quickly head out. He leaves the line and starts to follow me. I pick up my pace, and so does he.

Should I run?

I can run.

"Marley?"

Is he calling my name?

"Marley, wait up."

I walk faster.

"Chill," he calls out. "I just want to talk to you." I slow down and he jogs over to me. "My name's Brad," he says.

"What do you want?" My voice cracks. Of all the Gorn, he hits the hardest. I look around to see if this is an ambush.

"I just wanted to tell you that to go after Digger, you gotta be tough. Even we won't touch him. I gotta respect you for that."

I nod. "Yeah, whatever."

There's an awkward silence. He looks nervous. "Hey, I hope you know that when I hit you, it's nothing personal."

"Nothing personal." I gawk. "It's not personal that you hit me? I don't get it. Of everyone at school, why me?"

Brad shrugs. "Don't flatter yourself. It's not just you. There are lots of others. But mostly you 'cause you don't do anything. You just take it. So we dish it out." He shakes his head and for a moment I catch a glimpse of the look I've seen before on his face. Sadness. "I don't like it either," he says.

"Don't like what? Hitting me?"

"Yeah, that."

This is beyond weird. "Not to sound ignorant," I tell him, "but why don't you just stop?"

Suddenly, Brad starts laughing like a maniac. "Oooh, that's a good one."

"Well, why not? You don't like hitting me. I don't like getting hit. Hello? I see this as a win-win situation."

"Listen, I've tried to get it to stop," Brad tells me. He tugs on his collar. "I even made an anonymous call to Haycorn that day we slaughtered you."

Brad the Gorn made that phone call?

"Why would you do that? Wouldn't it be easier just to stop hitting me?"

As a couple of kids from school near, Brad puts his head down until they pass. "It's not that simple," he says when he looks up. "I can't explain it. It's just that, well, it's what we do, okay? If I want to be one of the guys, I gotta do it too. If I don't, they'll call me a coward and turn on me. I thought that Haycorn would be able to figure out it was us and make us stop. But he's too dense —"

Just then, something happens to Brad. He straightens up and his face contorts. "I'm sorry, but I gotta do this."

Before I can ask him what he's talking about, he slugs me in the stomach. As I keel over, I can hear the other two Gorn calling, "Good one!" as Brad runs toward them, laughing.

Yes. It's official. The world has turned upside down.

CAPTAIN'S LOG

The unexplained is suddenly explained, making the Gorn even more confusing than ever.

59.

It's morning. Digger is waiting for me at the corner. "Hey, Marley."

"Hey, Digger."

"I have something to ask you."

"Okay, what?"

"Do you want to be a Roadrunner?" When I hesitate, Digger explains. "Those are my guys. We all have Roadrunner jackets and do stuff together and everything. Do you want in?"

Cedra drives by and honks her horn. I wave to her, then face Digger. "Thanks, but I'm sort of already in a group."

For a moment, Digger looks disappointed. "Sure. Whatever," he says, straightening up.

"How are things at home?" I ask. His nose is looking better.

His jaw tenses. "Fine," he says.

"Does he hit you a lot?"

There is a silence between us that stretches out until the signal changes color again.

"Naw," he finally says as traffic rushes past us. "Just when I mess up. I deserve it. Does your dad ever hit you?"

I shake my head. "No, never."

A woman with a baby in a stroller walks past us, but neither of us moves. Digger fumbles with the zipper on his jacket and pulls it all the way up to his neck. He looks around, then asks, "Does he yell at you and make you feel worthless?"

"My dad and I get along really well. My mom too."

"You don't know how lucky you are," Digger says softly. "I wish I were you."

Digger Ronster wishes he were Marley Sandelski? We must have been sucked into a black hole when I wasn't looking, because it sure seems like we're in an alternate universe. I may not be sure of what's going on, but I do know one thing. I'm not scared of Digger anymore.

"Hey," I tell him, "if you ever need to get away, you can always hang out with me at the Rialto. We don't even have to tell anyone, if you don't want to."

"I may do that sometime," he says.

I reach into my pocket and pull something out. "Here, you can have this."

"Captain Kirk?" Digger says, staring at the action figure.

"I carry him around for good luck, but he's yours if you want him. He's a good guy."

For a moment, I think that Digger is going to laugh at me. But instead, he slips Captain Kirk in his pocket. "Thanks, Marley," he says. "I could use someone like Kirk on my side."

CAPTAIN'S LOG

Former foe now a friend?

I didn't sleep well last night. First, I was nervous because of the oral report I have to give today in McKenna's class. And second, Lavender played this really confusing song called "Muskrat Love" about these two muskrats named Susie and Sam who like to dance and eat bacon, and it made me think about Emily, even though we're not muskrats, and I don't dance, and I'm not sure if she even likes bacon. It still hurts when I see her, so whenever she's around, I just run away.

I'm in history right now, and we've been going alphabetically for the reports, which means I'm near the end. This is the third day we've been doing this. The girl before me gives her speech on the Bill of Rights. Everyone is struggling to stay awake, even her.

Digger was supposed to go before me, but he's not in class today. I wonder if he's really sick, or just avoiding giving a speech. I hope he's okay. I've been thinking a lot about Digger. Every time I relive the moment his father hit him, it feels like I'm being hit again too. I know he doesn't want anyone to know, but Digger's secret is tearing me apart. Maybe I'll tell Mom. Yes, I'll talk to my mother. She'll know what to do.

"Marley Sandelski, you're up next!" Ms. McKenna says.

My palms start sweating. I stand up. Julie yawns. "I need a minute," I say as I grab my backpack and bolt out the door.

I can hear Ms. McKenna calling out my name.

The hallway is empty. I could just take off right now and run away — but instead, I get ready and then step back into the room. A couple kids snicker. Ms. McKenna's eyes light up. I stride up to the front of the room and hold a hundred-dollar bill in the air. Well, okay, not a real one, but a picture of one.

"Everyone knows what this is," I begin. "But what do you know about the man on the hundred-dollar bill?" The last time I wore a costume in school I nearly died at the hands of the Gorn. But today, no one is out to kill me, and instead of being embarrassed, I feel at home in the brown velvet jacket with gold buttons. I slip on the glasses.

"His name is Benjamin Franklin, and not only was he one of the Founding Fathers of America, but he created the first public lending library and the first fire department. Franklin also invented the lightning rod, rocking chair, bifocals like the ones I'm wearing, and swim fins . . ."

When my report ends I bask in the enthusiastic cheering and applause. So what if it's only from Ms. McKenna?

"Marley has done a marvelous job of bringing history to life," she tells the class. "And I would like to continue that. Since we're done with our oral reports, and tomorrow's the last day of school before winter break, I was going to debut a vacation rap I just wrote." Students look sideways at each other and grimace. "But instead, I have an even better surprise . . . War Balls!" she shrieks. "Let's hear it for War Balls!"

No one moves.

"War Balls," Ms. McKenna explains as she passes them out. "These are a dessert that the soldiers ate during the Revolutionary War. Deep-fried dough rolled in sugar and cinnamon." They look like doughnut holes.

I'm a little scared as I take a tiny bite of my War Ball — then I smile. Ms. McKenna is right. They are great. No one's making fun of her now.

At lunchtime I'm not too hungry since I had five War Balls — Ms. McKenna slipped me some extra ones when class was over. Ramen is hovering over Max as she pops the lid off of her lunch. "Well?" he asks.

"Penne pesto with shaved parmesan cheese. You?"

"Shrimp ramen," he answers as he stares at her lunch.

"I've never known anyone who loves noodles as much as you," she tells him.

"Love noodles?" Ramen looks shocked. "I hate them!"

"Then why do you eat them every day?"

"Because they're cheap and my mom buys them by the case at Costco. Who'd willingly eat this stuff?"

"I would," Max says.

"Really?"

"I love ramen noodles, but my mom refuses to buy them," Max explains, adding, "She's a foodie."

"What's that?" asks Ramen,

"You know, a food snob," says Max.

"I want to be a foodie," Ramen announces.

"Then switch," I say. "Why don't you two switch lunches?"

Max and Ramen fall silent. Then slowly smiles cross their faces as they trade lunches.

"Hey," I say as they are both blissfully eating, "I'm thinking of proposing a *Star Trek* movie marathon to my dad. What do you think?"

"I'd rather see a Batman marathon," Max says as she slurps up a noodle.

"I'd rather go to a *Star Wars* marathon," Ramen says before taking another mouthful of his penne pesto.

I take a War Ball out of the bag and bite into it as I think about the marathon.

The *Star Wars* vs. *Star Trek* battle has heated up again, with Max insisting that Batman is the best, and no one listening to her. Everyone in AV Club is debating which marathon would draw the biggest crowd.

"Mr. Jiang!" Patrick calls out. "You can settle this once and for all. What's better, *Star Wars* or *Star Trek*?"

"Or Batman?" Max shouts.

Ramen, Max, Troy, Patrick, and I all stop and look at Mr. Jiang when he says, "Every day you kids come in here with the same old arguments, and every day you disagree. I've been waiting for the moment when you'd ask me my opinion."

"Well, what is it?" Troy presses. "*Star Trek* or *Star Wars*?"

"Or Batman?" adds Max.

"I'm going to tell you, and I'm only going to say this once, okay?" Mr. Jiang says.

We all nod solemnly.

Mr. Jiang clears his throat and hesitates. The suspense is killing us. "Superman!" he announces with a grin.

Chaos breaks loose as everyone begins yelling.

"Superman doesn't even count! He has superpowers. That's cheating!" Troy protests.

"Yeah," Patrick cries. "He's not even a real person, like Luke and Han!"

"Or Bruce Wayne," Max points out.

"Superpowers are a cop-out," Ramen adds. "Our guys use their wits and their brains —"

". . . and their Batmobile," Max jumps in. "Superman is not even in the same category as Batman!"

As we spend the rest of sixth period arguing, Mr. Jiang leans back in his chair and chuckles.

CAPTAIN'S LOG

The planets are in alignment.

61.

One more class to go before winter break, then two whole weeks of freedom. I'm going to be busy, though. Last night Dad agreed to have the First Annual Rialto Klingons, Kenobi, and Capes Marathon. Just think: *Star Trek*, *Star Wars*, and Batman, together for one film festival! I don't think that's ever been done before. We're also going to have panel discussions and debates, and who knows? Maybe we can get some of the stars to show up.

Max and Ramen are going to help out, plus Troy and Patrick said they'd pitch in too. We're making posters and stuff and I'm going to ask the local businesses to put them up. Mr. Min from RadioShack has already said he would, and so did Dave at the Dinosaur Farm.

As I head to sixth period my head is full of ideas, when the Gorn suddenly materialize out of nowhere. Before I can react, I'm boxed in. They have greedy looks on their faces, like they're going to devour me and spit out my bones.

"You think you're so tough just because you beat up Digger," the Gorn leader hisses. "Well, we're going to find out how tough you really are."

The small Gorn laughs as Brad looks away. Kids slow down. Some stop and stare. Before long, there's a crowd.

"Is the little lady scared?" the Gorn leader taunts.

I grimace as they shove me against the wall. I can't run. My WWSD has disappeared, and I don't even have Captain Kirk with me. Where's Kirk when I need him?

"Hit him," the Gorn leader tells Brad.

My heart is racing.

WWSD? What would Spock do?

WWKD? What would Kirk do? What would he do? What should I do?

WWMD? WWMD? WWMD?

What would Marley do?

Time stops while I remember when the Gorn first started punching me. I remember when they slammed me into my locker. I remember when they beat me up and laughed. They're laughing now.

My eyes flutter open. There is still a fist in front of my face. The Gorn are still laughing. More kids are gathered around. Some look excited because they are going to see me get beat up. Others look curious. One boy, who looks like he's about eight years old, looks scared. He grips his books to his chest as if for protection.

Brad is holding me by the collar. The other Gorn are egging him on. "Just hit him," the small Gorn yells. "What are you waiting for?"

"Do it!" says the leader. He looks at me and grins. "What's the matter, Sandelski, you chicken?"

I think of my father holed up in the projection booth telling me about Karl Bricknell. Clearly, this is a Kobayashi Maru, a no-win situation. If I fight them, I will lose. If they fight me, I will lose. Any fight, and I will lose. There's nothing I can do . . . or wait . . . is there?

I've got it! Like Kirk in the new *Star Trek* movie, I'll change the rules.

Brad is still staring at me. There is no joy on his face. The Gorn leader is squawking now, and so is the little Gorn. It's so loud it's echoing in my head.

"Leave me alone," I say softly. "Leave. Me. Alone. Leave me alone." With each breath I take, I get louder, until I start to drown out the squawking. Suddenly, I am shouting like a maniac, "LEAVE ME ALONE!"

Brad blinks rapidly, then releases me like I'm radioactive. The Gorn look surprised. So does everyone else. I face the crowd. "This isn't a spectator sport," I say as I plead my case. "We can't let them get away with this. If you just stand there and watch, then you're just as bad as they are. C'mon, someone say something. They can't fight all of us!"

There is total silence.

I have never felt so alone in my life. I'm going to die and these kids are just going to let it happen.

Suddenly, someone pushes through the crowd. "Leave him alone!"

It's Max!

Ramen is hiding behind her. He chirps up, "Be a buddy, not a bully!"

Even though the three of us are probably going to get decimated, I break into a grin. Max and Ramen do the same.

Then the most amazing thing happens. Another voice cries, "Leave him alone!"

I whip around and see the boy from P.E., the one with the thick glasses. A couple of other kids join in, then more and more. Soon the hallway is echoing with kids yelling, "Leave him alone!"

"Go away!"

"Cowards!"

The Gorn look confused, then nervous as the crowd pushes forward, yelling. Nerds, geeks, and dorks of every size and shape have materialized. The Gorn begin to pale, then they take off down the hall, first walking, then running. It's like the Battle of Trenton! The enemy has been contained. Everyone cheers. The Gorn have disappeared.

I look around. There's electricity in the air as kids head to class, chattering about what just happened. Who are all these people? Where did they come from? None of them look familiar. I've never noticed them before. How can that be? I thought I was the only invisible one at this school.

"Well, I certainly showed those bullies," Ramen boasts as he puffs out his chest. "Buddy, they won't be bothering you any time soon."

Max pats me on the back. "As Batman has said, 'Criminals are a superstitious, cowardly lot.' Come on, Marley, we don't want to be late to AV Club."

"You guys go on ahead," I say. "I'll be right there."

I need to catch my breath. My heart is still racing. I feel exhilarated.

After Max and Ramen take off, I notice the small skinny boy lingering. His brown hair is all choppy, like he cut it himself, and his pants are way too short. He's wearing a Spiderman shirt. "Hey, thanks," he says. He sounds nervous.

"For what?"

"Well, first you showed Digger who's boss, and now you stood up to those bullies. Marley, you give the rest of us hope."

"You know who I am?"

"Of course. You're Marley Sandelski." The tardy bell rings. "Well, I'd better go," he says. "See you around, Marley."

"Wait," I call after him. "What's your name?"

"Jacob," he says.

I watch Jacob get smaller as he races to class. Mr. Jiang's going to be mad that I'm late and Haycorn may even haul me in for being tardy — but I have something I need to do.

I turn to the first page of my Captain's Log. In two weeks it'll be a new year. Maybe it's time for a new word, and a new me.

I take out a pen and cross out "invisible." Then above it I write . . .

INVINCIBLE
~~invisible~~

ABOUT THE AUTHOR

Lisa Yee is the author of three previous books about the kids of Rancho Rosetta: *Millicent Min, Girl Genius*; *Stanford Wong Flunks Big-Time*; and *So Totally Emily Ebers*. On one of her many school visits, a reader asked what happened to Marley from *Stanford Wong*, which inspired her to tell his story here.

Lisa lives, eats, writes, and blogs — sometimes all at once — in South Pasadena, California, which may or may not be the basis for Rancho Rosetta. Please visit her website at www.lisayee.com.